The Enigma Trilogy

WORLDS WITHIN WORLDS

ROBYN YOUNG

Fulton Books, Inc.
Meadville, PA

Published by Fulton Books 2022

ISBN 978-1-63985-209-3 (paperback)
ISBN 978-1-63985-210-9 (digital)

Printed in the United States of America

CHAPTER 1

Just Passing Through

The end was the beginning of a new journey. The last seconds of my life felt like an eternity all in one moment of letting go.

With a cold metal of the pistol jammed into the back of my head, my cheek sunk into the pavement, and thoughts ran through my head as fast as my whole life could flash before my eyes.

The voice inside whispered, "This second you get to let everything you ever thought was wrong or right go." I knew then this was the end of me as I knew it. I had to leave my family and loved ones here for me to move on to the next step of consciousness. This was it. I had to accept that I had nothing to hold onto once the gun was fired.

My heart was beating so fast I prayed I would pass out before feeling the pain of the bullet in my brain. My sight turned pitch black as the loudest *bang* echoed through vibrations of my eardrums, and I felt nothing at all.

I could still hear a high-pitched ringing as I saw what was once my body lying in the middle of the road, looking around, feeling everything that was, along with everything that came to be. If all the love in the universe could be in one place at one time, that's what this was. I felt every fiber of my being with all the potential of every soul's capacity of acceptance, encouragement, and forgiveness.

I stood by my family at the service they gathered for, to bury my old body. I could feel their pain of loss, confusion of why, emptiness, and fear of how life would go on. Although I no longer had emotions to shed a tear, I could send thoughts of love back to them, having already understood the pain of being human.

The sun broke through the clouds, illuminating an energy surrounding me. I peered around as I saw my grandma and father standing by my side. No words were said in a language I had ever known except for feelings of love and acceptance, along with a sense of celebrating achievements with an embrace that no one should ever be afraid of.

I linked frequencies with them, leaving the scene as if by the speed of light, passing through vortexes like wormholes of space and time. I knew I was going to meet something, someone familiar. I could feel infinite love, a love that was unfathomable to the human consciousness.

Inside this dimension far from Earth and yet close enough to realize the connection was paper thin, I found myself in a well-known state of being surrounded by energies I was already accustomed to. Others gathered around in support of my stewardship report that I felt were there to absorb my energy, to recognize it in our next life.

It was no surprise to me that spirits connected to humans still living on earth were there to stand witness as well. My ancestors, people that I hurt, people that helped me, that died for me, I inspired or bullied, and everyone that my presence affected by my life story were by my side. It was an instant understanding from the ripples that I had created through my ego, spiritual and physical actions had an expanding effect on the human evolution. I felt all life forces in connection with one another feeding and flowing consciousness effortlessly.

A unanimous conscious decision placed me in a realm of closing gaps I left behind. From that point on, I spread myself out to every footstep of my path, gathering information from the energy that built up matter. From all thoughts of my human existence, I was able to tap into energy source and laugh with my family and friends as they shared stories about my humanness; reach out to them with love and understanding as they released sadness of missing my presence around.

They felt my thoughts on their behalf, but most brushed it off as if they were crazy to feel energy and insight they didn't see with their eyes.

Crossing the boundary of free will was not an option, only love and acceptance, knowing that being human could be contradicting at times. Whenever anyone asked for my presence, I knocked on the door and spoke to them through their thoughts. They could hear the knock; they let the thoughts pass through them, and yet they dismissed it all as they allowed fear to stand in front of them.

The feeling of being an outcast for humans in this world is all too common. Everyone feels it, and little do we all know that we have already embraced that feeling, labeling it with negative emotions attached that latch onto us, plant a seed inside us. Then when we recognize that feeling with someone else, we shame them, not knowing we are shaming ourselves in the same manner. Feelings and thoughts are hard to distinguish for humans, but very important for the healing process. It's a matter of letting go that opens the door to new feelings.

With time extended in the spiritual realm, I was able to accomplish a month's number of chores all in an earth day's work to help everyone I could stay on course. Like planting seeds and growing crops in the open fields, everyone was bound to grow and bloom eventually.

It was a powerful feeling to be in love and forgiveness as we cheered on all of creation to take on a life as a human, animal, and life matter that could feel.

One by one I witnessed close loved ones let go of their human and animal bodies and welcomed them back to the other side of the picture, the other process of creation.

Weaving through parallels, connecting the dots, we moved like a system where all are instilled with the power to be what was in the nature of their own evolvement—like time stood still with energy in motion, the peace in revolving movement, not even air to stand in our way or slow us down. Nothing in the possibility of everything—that's us.

I brought along my sense of humor like any other human soul that understood the twisted humor of humans. Sometimes hiding keys, spilling coffee, and riling up pets helped humans to stop and slow down for moments when they got ahead of themselves or got stuck in their own way of thinking, correlating the alignment with actions to throw them off their games, so to speak. Some things were just meant to happen for human evolvement, and sometimes life distracted us from remembering that we all signed up for this in one form or another.

After a certain amount of mending and healing, I was transported back to the origin. Another mission had come up for me of importance that called for my individual expertise. Without a doubt, I agreed and pack my so-called bags.

I sensed a connection to a body of matter like an oven timer that was soon to go off. An excitement of anticipation built up as loved ones gathered to bid me another farewell.

A new beginning awaited where the end of my wholeness joined back together for the spiraling journey through space and time. Like animal instincts, I knew what to do.

GOOD GOD

It's hard to believe love has an enemy and love is all that is.
It's hard to believe fiction is reality in fear of justice. Do you
believe in God? Do you believe in the good inside us?
Looking for love in all the wrong places / the search is
over when you see God in all the faces through the eyes of
your heart—the good is God expressing art inside us.
It's hard to believe we've come all this way and love
is all we have. It's hard to believe holding back love
today is what holds us back. Do you believe in good?
Do you believe compassion's misunderstood?
I believe that love is true. I believe there is good in me and you—
rush to the sun, the light illuminating the crown of everyone.
The good, the God we speak of—the only
truth we have—the only truth is Love.

CHAPTER 2

The Birth

Spiraling down a psychedelic vortex, energy was building up like a snowball rolling down a mountain. An orb of energy shot through the sky; a shooting star relocated, aligning with the new orbit of stars in the cosmos, blazing a new trail, opening portals all the way to the earth's surface.

It's a thought in motion, a feeling broken down to molecules flowing through the human brain, triggering a reaction from energy in motion. The vibration stretched throughout the realm in thoughts, feelings, and matter, balancing all minds, bodies, and spirits connected by circuits of the whole.

It felt like I was on the edge of my seat, being pushed off by a force behind me more powerful than I could drag my feet against. Or rather, I was being pulled to the light at the end of the tunnel. Either way, intensity was building up like a heart beating on the verge of a panic attack.

A mother was in labor, with excruciating pain being released into the environment, dispersing into the air that all humans, species, and nature shared. Every being would feel this birth and wouldn't understand, recognize, and most likely not even acknowledge as a universal gift, a feeling, and opportunity of healing the unit.

In one ear and out the other, in one breath and out for the next person to deal with or ignore while they were caught up and distracted by fixed beliefs that outside sources fed them once upon a time. And now they replayed in their heads like that *Groundhog* movie.

One more big push, one more scream, releasing weakness from this female body enduring pain, overwhelming for an unconscious mindset; and this mother conquered it, focusing on the want, desire, love, and worth of this brand-new child squinting at the lights surrounding him.

It felt like a rubber band was stretched out and snapped back into place, like it was hit so hard the shock erased any visual knowledge or memory of where I just was, only muscle memory in my brain from past lives with a body of a seed that had been planted underground and pulled back out. I was now figuring out how to survive as I went.

My only rope of security was snapped. Suddenly alone here in a new place, and I was feeling something. This little body was convulsing. I got the quivers, and I wanted my rope back. These other big humans were mumbling loud noises ever since I got here. I couldn't make out the sounds, but I knew that they were the ushers to this new life I had just begun.

The voices seemed to be coming from behind the white shields in front of the planet-shaped domes on top of their human forms. I recognized something on the planets, just above those white shields, twin portals, of eyes staring back at me like doorways opening and closing really quickly but mostly staying open for me to see through.

Hey, I remember you! I passed by that galaxy on my way here. That gamma-ray burst blew cosmic dust into my orb as I shuttled by on my way here. It felt like a distant memory now, but still a familiar sense to my comfort.

This body felt cold. My limbs were hanging as though I was floating, and this body with the twin portals had pulled me in close, stalling me in the sky. My natural human instincts were familiar with gravity forces, and I was feeling nervous with this detachment. Oh, I was moving through the air again.

I could see the small portals of where I came from reflected back by all these other beings around me. A beautiful woman radiating a comfort of belonging held out her limbs, embracing my body. I locked eyes with her. It felt a world away, and yet I could reach out with my body and touch her.

I had traveled to a world within another world, I figured out as I stared into her eye portals. I missed being in that world, and at the same time, I was glad she was still here with me, holding me in a different way. It's like I moved out of my childhood home and into another home with a broader view.

"Hi," I heard her say. "I'm your new mommy." All I heard was blah, blah, blah. But inside I felt she was happy to see me too as a brighter glow surrounded her face when she smiled at me. I snuggled my body into her chest, to the familiar vibration of the beating of her heart and thoughts. *Mom, please don't let me go.*

I remembered my first home. Well, glimpses of it. I remembered feeling scared when loud noises came out of my father. Soon after, my mother would come into my room and hold me while she cried. Whenever she would do that, I felt mixed emotions. I felt comforted to be in her arms, and at the same time, I could feel her worrying, questioning, almost as though she was silently praying to know what to do. I heard my own voices telling me to stay calm, keep breathing, and trust in my mom's love for me, and together we will be all right. I liked those voices.

When it got dark at night, things were different. I never looked forward to night sleeps because no one understood my terrors that came into my room. It felt like every time I would fall asleep, I would wake up suddenly, not being able to move my body. I tried to scream for my mom as I watched disfigured men in black come in and hover over me.

I knew they were coming when I started smelling a wet mildew as though water had been trickling down stone walls of an old dungeon. I felt like they came to take me away from my mom forever, and I wasn't physically strong enough to change it. They fed me an unfamiliar, unnerving energy, and in return, they took it back to take charge or get charged.

I felt like I had a chance if only I could kick and scream at them. That usually gets my mom's attention, but I couldn't when they were there. They were like bullies who just wanted to watch me cry, wet myself, and shake with an overwhelming fear that I didn't understand. They even smiled when I would struggle the most as though they were thanking me for gifting them with that pleasure, that energy fuel.

One particular night, when I was feeling helpless against them, just before dread completely took over me, I heard one of those soft voices telling me to remember my mom holding me earlier on that day. It was a close memory, so it felt easy to tap in to.

We were sitting on a chair in front of the living-room window while she read my favorite book to me called *Love You Forever* by Robert Munsch. Remembering this, I felt my body starting to get warmer as the comfort of my mother's love took over my thoughts.

One of the men reached out, pulling a green light from my body space. They never touched or hurt me, just gave me a sense that nothing else ever did or could.

I wiggled my body free from entrapment and shouted as loud as I could, "Mom, Mom!" I was overwhelmed with tears falling down my cheeks, gasping for air as I continued to call out for my mother, and they disappeared as she ran into the room.

I never told my mom about the men in my room, and she never asked. She just held me, assuring that everything was okay and that she was always here for me.

In This Together

I thought I was in it to win it / projecting, I see a new
way to spin it. What good are memories with no one to
share it? What good is love if no one will spare it?
Our love goes on forever / bearing the scars / raising the bar /
walking on water to the stars. We're in this together / to warm
the hearts/ of those in the dark / hand in hand we play our part.
Peace of mind—imagination will find a way. Leave thoughts
behind—recreation of a new day. Fight for love. Live and die
for love. The new world rises above in love. See it through. Keep
believing what the angels see in you. That's the only truth. It's love.
I am what you expect from me. You are what I believe I see.
Change your mind—change reality—change your perception
of you and me. I am what I am. I am in love. I am free.
Come out and see… We're in this together—sharing love, we'll
rise above. It's now or never. We have today. We have each other.
We're in this together—it's never too late to break out forever.
Whatever it takes—we're in this together / together in love.

CHAPTER 3

Triggers

That one night changed my life forever. Not only did the men never return again, I found out that I had a secret power against them. I knew that the next time they were going to try and scare me, I would think about my mom hugging and kissing me, and I would scare them back; but they never again gave me a chance to show them my magic I was ready to use on them.

That night also made my angry father leave forever. At four years old, most of my days were spent following my mom around the house, watching her clean, talk on the phone, look at her papers on the table, go to the stores with her, and occasionally I would watch TV.

One particular day in the fall, I was in the backyard, swiping at the falling leaves in the air with my sword, preparing for the night watchers and feeling very confident with my newfound skills. I was crushing those dead leaves, and in my head, I pictured slicing up those scary men to pieces.

As I stopped to look around at all the leaves accumulating on the ground, catching my breath, I heard the front door slam. I tend to freeze up when I get scared; even though I was feeling stronger and braver than I have ever felt, I wasn't expecting this.

My dad was yelling loud enough for the neighbors to hear. He said something about losing his job and that it was my mom's fault. Then I heard him say my name. My mom liked to call me Mickey, but my dad would refer to me as Michael. He was so angry about me crying for my mom at night that it would keep him up too.

In a way, I understood how he felt because I, too, was angry that my sleep had been interrupted. He was also mad that my mom spent time with me and took care of me, which confused my way of thinking. I was grateful for my mom being there for me. At four years old, she had been my only friend. Besides the voices in my head, I didn't have anyone else, and she fed me, so that was a plus.

I was confused about him not wanting her to be with me. He said that she loved me more than him and everything was her fault. That translated in my head to be my fault. I knew I needed my mom. I wouldn't know what to do without her, and this man said that we ruined his life because she loved me.

I walked up to the back patio so I could get a better picture through the screen door. I felt a knot in my stomach, like my nerves wanted my body to purge ill emotions out of my body that just lost a war of love. My mother said very few words as he brought some bags to the front door. I couldn't make out what she said. She wasn't as loud as my dad.

He opened the front door and turned around to take one last look at us. I could see through the screen door, past the dining and living room, into his eyes. Through those twin portals, darkness twirled inside, stretching out, circling his whole body. It wasn't a happy look, to say the least, and at that moment I knew the scary night watchers were leaving with him.

He picked up his bags and *slammed* the door behind him. I flinched as the door shut, even though I saw it coming. I didn't like loud sudden noises, but that was the last time I saw my father.

Tears ran down my mom's face. As I came in through the back door, I felt a sigh of relief. These were tears like a rainstorm at the perfect time of year that cleaned out the dirty, hazy air.

The house was brighter than I ever remembered it being. It was like the sun came out from behind clouds, pouring in light through the windows of the house. I reached out and hugged my mom. I felt like we had just won a battle that made us both want a nap, but we chose to celebrate like we always knew how to, embracing each other. I hugged her until the sunset that night.

It wasn't very long after that that my mom got the news of my father's death. The divorce wasn't finalized yet, so the police came knocking on our door.

It was in the early morning. I was sitting on the floor in front of the TV with a bowl of cereal and my G.I. Joes. I didn't get up, but I focused my ears on them over *Tom and Jerry* on the screen. I heard one police officer mention alcohol and driving off the road, along with the word *deceased*.

Although I didn't know what all that meant, I pictured it in my mind as clear as the TV in front of my eyes. I saw my dad's bloody, lifeless face resting on the steering wheel of his truck with an empty glass bottle on the floor of the passenger's side as water from a river was slipping through the cracks on the doors, filling up the cab.

I knew my father was dead, and even though I had grown used to him not being around—and it wasn't a happy place when he was—but some things you couldn't un-visualize, and I remembered that vision to this day.

The good news was, he left some money for my mother, just enough to buy a new house and put her through school. We agreed to leave those memories with that house and move on.

My mom got a great deal on an old Victorian home in an up-and-coming community. It was obvious at first sight to know that it must have been on a plantation, and the city took over the land, building new housing around it. There was a lot of history in that home, and those walls certainly knew how to talk to me. Fortunately, not in the same way as our last house did, so I knew we were upgrading.

My mom got a paralegal degree. It wasn't her first choice, but it paid the bills, and there was hope for her that she could make a difference in this world, as small as it may seem. She used to joke about her job with her friends. I remembered her describing her job, how she taught the lawyers how to lie in order to win their case. I knew my mom was a great woman, so that's all that mattered to me.

We made a lot of new memories in that house, and some felt like we had made them before. Déjà vu, perhaps, or something else in that realm of energy, had an effect on our daily lives.

I was around eight years old when I got up one night to use the bathroom. My mother had an early meeting the next morning, so we both went to sleep earlier than usual. With the house being bigger than anything that my mom and I needed, there were two extra guest bedrooms in the house being unoccupied. Or so I thought.

As I was walking down the hall to the bathroom, I saw something move in the corner of my eye.

Only the light of the full moon and stars shining through the windows cast down light in the house, from a hazy white to the deepest shades of grey fading into black, lining the corners down the hall.

I turned to see a blurry silhouette of a mother holding a little boy's hand, leading him in the guest bedroom at the end of the hallway. The boy turned his head, smiling at me, as they disappeared through the wall.

Chills ran up and down my body, but I didn't feel threatened. It was nothing like the fright I had known before, but a questionable curiousness of something I still didn't quite understand, and I knew that no one I knew here on earth had the answers I was looking for. I did my business in the bathroom and went back to bed.

For the next few years, I would catch quick glimpses of the boy around the house and in the yard. I grew older while he stayed the same age until he didn't come around anymore, like a memory slowing fading into the past, and I was moving on into a new life in high school.

Mom and I had a routine down. She went to work as I went to school. I worked part-time at a retail store in the mall on the weekends to save up for my own car and help out any way I could. Whenever Mom and I would both have an evening off, we make sure we had dinner together and watched a movie of her choice. Chick flicks kept a spark lit for my mom not to give up hope for a long-lasting romance in her future, which came true my senior year.

I was on the varsity basketball team, and one evening after a victory over our rivals, we went out for pizza to celebrate. My mom, being as supportive as she is, came along and really hit it off with my basketball coach, Tim Hansen.

As far as I knew, Coach Hansen was a decent man. He had an overachiever for a daughter in her sophomore year, and he always motivated just enough to keep me at arm's length, as I later understood why. It was rumored that he had a son close to my age who was diagnosed with bipolar disorder, something about a mishap with his meds that led him to commit suicide. He didn't talk about it, and we didn't ask.

They continued dating for months through my graduation and the summer after. I never put in for colleges, and I turned down a few basketball scholarships. The only future I saw for myself was in the army, so I didn't make a plan B. I didn't know why, and I couldn't explain how I knew it was the next step for me. I couldn't tell if I wanted to be in the army or the army wanted me to be there. Either way, it was calling me, and I answered.

It was tough for me to pack my bags for basic. At the same time, Coach Hansen had my mom smiling again, so I felt comforted leaving my mom in good hands. She was happy.

Coach Hansen came over that morning to be with my mother after we say our farewells. Neither I nor my mom were good at goodbyes, so we did what we knew how to do and said goodbye at the front door.

My longtime friend, Josh, signed up the same week, so we would drive out together. He waited in his car by the mailbox in uniform as I hugged my mother and shook Coach's hand. It surprised me when he pulled my hand in for a hug. I felt nerves convulsing in his stomach as he held me close. He was struggling to stuff emotions, holding back tears, so I let go before it got uncomfortable. I was too busy noticing his emotions to express my own, leaving with an empty goodbye.

They stood together on the front porch, waving, as Josh and I drove out of the neighborhood. Like a blazing comet, I didn't look back to see the traces of energy I was leaving behind. We were off on a mission, maybe as stubborn, prideful young men or faithful servants… That was all a matter of perspective, but there we went, no questions asked.

This world had been at war for years now. Hell, even decades. So immediately after basic, we shipped off to the other side of the world.

"This ain't nothing like *Call of Duty*, eh, Mick?" It was typical of Josh to say something like that abruptly following a massive blow of rocks and debris from the corner of the roof we were staged on that had just exploded off to our right. It was a squared-off building made of stucco or who knows what these foreigners used to make their shit. The flat tops on the roof made it easier for stakeouts, and being the tallest building in the city, it gave us the best view from all angles.

The problem with that was, we were the biggest target. Well, there was always going to be trial and error in war, but I didn't have time to think about that when we were caught up in enemy fire. It seemed like every time I thought about any memory, my mom, or start to question if I was going to make it out of here alive, I got shot at, so I stopped thinking beyond right here, right now. And right now, a car bomb exploded right in front of the building we were perched up on, like baby birds in a nest waiting for their mom to come back with some worm guts for us.

The ringing in my ears from the blast was so loud I didn't get around to responding to Josh's sarcasm. I covered my ears in reaction to the eruption and turned my head away. As I reached down for my gun I dropped in the quake of the burst, I saw Josh, half of Josh. One side of his body had been blown to pieces along with the building. What was left of Josh was dropping to the ground of the roof behind me.

I quickly tossed my gun back down, reaching out to Josh.

"Josh, no!"

I wasn't there to catch him in time before the rest of Josh hit the roof. Part of his face was still intact. His left eye opened so wide as though it was very much aware of the explosion. I had never seen anything like it. I had never felt so much guilt and remorse in all my life. What about his mom? What about his family? What about Josh?

Bullets whistled passed my head. I couldn't grasp my feelings, let alone my gun to shoot back. I felt like I was surrounded by evil, and I hadn't felt so petrified since I was a little kid. My captain was yelling in my face, but all the sounds were muffled like a distant background of riots. Every fiber of my body went into shock. Staring passed my captain screaming at me, I saw a man in a window of the building across the street, aiming a missile launcher in our direction.

Suddenly this feeling seemed all too familiar. The look in the man's eyes radiated a darkness I had seen before. It felt like it was reaching out to me or even waving to me with a sadistic smile.

That was the last thing I remembered, which brought me here today at the VA hospital back in the States. My leg shattered. They said they had no choice but to amputate, and I'd have a prosthetic in no time. I had a few broken ribs, and the shrapnel wounds were still healing, but that's not what hurt. Sure, my whole body was in excruciating pain, but it's my brain that couldn't shut down this visual rampage repeating over and over in my head like a broken record.

When my body got well enough to be released, my mom brought me home. I refused help from her as we walked up the porch steps to the door where Coach Hansen, or shall I say, my new step-dad and sister waited hesitantly in the doorway. My face cringed with every step up, leaning on my cane for support.

The last memory I had of this porch was the last time I saw my mom. I hadn't looked at her since she picked me up, and the whole ride home, I didn't remember much. I made that the last memory I had of my mother, and it felt like a distant memory getting harder to hold on to as I kept remembering the shadow lurking in the man's eyes that killed my best friend and tried to take me out as well.

I looked into that same shadow in my eyes as they stared back at me in the mirror of the bathroom, disgusted. As I shook it off and came to, my fist was already flying through the air and shattered that reflective glass. I couldn't live like this. I couldn't live with this inside me.

I walked out of the bathroom feeling emptier than I ever had. Everyone else had stopped what they were doing when they heard the glass break and ran past me in the doorway to see what happened.

Immediately they went to cleaning it up, asking what was wrong, but my words couldn't come close to expressing what was wrong with me. Something foreign was inside that didn't belong, infecting my being.

I walked into my bedroom, locked the door behind me, took my .45mm out from my dresser drawer, and sat on my bed. Without another thought in my mind, I aimed at the darkness and pulled the trigger.

GOOD ENOUGH

I can't take it back. I can't make it right. Whatever happened
won't happen again tonight. Chasing the dream,
is it in me? Am I good enough to face myself? Will
I ever be good enough for my own company?
I see myself—the best I can be. Am I good enough as me?
Take me as I am. Take me right now. I'll do it right this
time. I'll do it right now. I'll make you mine. Will that be
good enough? Will you be satisfied? Will it be good enough
to say goodbye and let the past lay where it may?
Am I good enough today? Good enough my
way? Just feeling good enough to say…
Take one step forward. Take one step toward me. Take a
leap. Reach for me. The dream was never far away. Waking
up every day facing the truth—I was born this way.
A black sheep enlightened by the deep sleepers—
good enough to keep the light on.
What can I say? I'm not taking it back. It's taking me away.

CHAPTER 4

Resolution

I couldn't tell you everything that happened during the spiritual healing process behind the veil. I could only tell you from my personal
feelings and reflections. All other information was what we call "protected" by universal laws that spirit guides vowed to keep secret until
I reached that level of enlightenment. "Line upon line," they said.
That was a spiritual bond that could never be broken.

What I could share with you was that karma forgot no one.
Healing guilt and shame was the hardest aspect of being human, and
holding on to consciousness was the name of the game in terms of
evolution. It didn't work when you took it upon yourself to end your
life. It didn't get easier. The pain came from thoughts, and thoughts
didn't go away after you died for some of us. It's like trying to drink
your problems away, but if you didn't face them and heal them, they
would be waiting for you in the morning when you woke up with
a hangover, not feeling well enough to face and deal with them yet
again; and it's a constant cycle until it was done.

It took courage and faith in a resolution you might not see in
front of you, but there was always a solution to any challenge or fear
made up by the human mind. It's an illusion that you decide the
outcome to. You just have to go through it. We're playing humans,
getting hired on to a job that we were trained to do in another life.

One of my spirit guides was named Ezekiel. Similar to the ghost
of Christmas past taking Ebenezer Scrooge on a journey to see a

glimpse of the effects he had on his community, I, too, was taken on my own journey.

God, as I understood, was pure energy, the power connecting all life, elements, the sun, the moon, and beyond; was everywhere and nowhere to be seen, formless; and was understandably nameless. I could feel in my essence, being stripped of my human form, that if "God" as we understood God had a form, gender, color, number, etc., the human race would egotistically create a name, intention, and power to it, inevitably finding a way to destroy it and claim possession, as seen in the world today. So was the world at war with God or against God?

This was the knowledge I wanted to take with me to contribute to the human evolvement. My human journey might appear to be a disgrace and worthless effort, but that was only a possibility, a fixed belief among infinite possibilities and ways of looking at it.

Like the nameless power over us all, the language spoken in the spiritual realm wasn't divided, labeled, or categorized to one specific way of communicating. Telepathy was universal. It was intention, feeling with an individual understanding to expand the connection through individual networks of the whole, such as thoughts or channeling. While taking this journey with Ezekiel, I asked about the darkness, fear, and evil presence in my bedroom as a child. Feeling still like a child, I wanted closure to my experience, closure of wounds not yet healed.

Ezekiel explained fears to me to my best understanding. He said, *The blood of your father and mother runs through your veins. It's inherited from their parents that didn't heal the pain when they were human. There is a choice at all times to choose love or fear. It's that simple.*

I watched myself as a small child slipping into sleep paralysis, and changing the course of my life in that moment, I chose to recall the love of my mother. I could feel the contrast of light and dark, love and fear, heavy weight and ethereal lightness that completed us as a whole. I felt whole again, a feeling I had forgotten as a human being involved in an illusion of others, believing that, somehow, they were different than me, made up of different matter, when the truth was, we were made up of the same soul. We were one consciousness. I felt an understanding and acceptance to all human lives feeling like lost souls in our own collective conscious. I felt love for all.

It's as though a burst of energy, like an electric wave, shot out of my body from all angles, rippling out through the walls, down the road, past the city, and onto disrupt the pattern of waves in the ocean; vibrating out past Earth, creating a current in the cosmos like a gust of wind directing asteroids and shooting stars; aligning into a different space and time.

That was the most empowering feeling I could take with me to do better next time. It was not just in knowing the difference I could make. Ezekiel also said, *It is through human eyes and residual energy in the bloodstream that sees fear as an enemy, as a demon, a frightening darkness, but look all around.*

Faster than the speed of light, the speed of thought brought us into the outer space of the earth where planets and stars aligned in orbit connected like a mathematical grid. I had never seen anything like it nor could I comprehend even being in the midst of it. I was in complete awe. Overtaken by this unfathomable sight, my orb sparkled with excitement, peace, and openness all encompassed in this infinite power source. (Who said you couldn't hold more than one frequency at a time?)

Nebulas, solar flares, and gamma-ray burst caught my attention, but Ezekiel shared his light on the space between. *An immature conscious sees darkness beyond matter.* Well, why did he have to say that? Now I'm focusing on that. He further explained, *Humans give power to words with intention and create a solid energy based on the influence of belief. When the earth was a much-simpler place with much less walls, division, and complexity, the word "evil" was used as meaning "unripe."*

That wisdom, resonating truth for me, lit my orb again. I could feel an electric current vibrating inside my energy field like human nerves aroused and stimulated by connecting to a new energy or combatable elements in chemistry.

Ezekiel, feeling the excitement of my newfound energy, felt it was the perfect moment to add more fuel to my fire. *Because of free will given to humans, there comes the possibility of misunderstanding, miscommunication, and mistakes that really aren't mistakes at* *another way of doing or not doing something. From this, sin has taken a new meaning as well. It went from a simple 'miss' for archers or anyone aiming at a target to a condemnation, shame, and a state of guilt that is to be believed that one has had developed in to a block in the paths of humans, a wall they claim as shame. So much emphasis and focus has claimed the power of so many lives that children are being born into an environment set up for a mental overload, shutdown, or breakdown.*

As Ezekiel explained the process gradually progressing, I viewed in on many lives on the earth and how they were being affected and infected by people around them. Like my ripple of love and courage, there, too, was a multitude of ripples happening at every moment on earth unseen to the human eyes.

Zooming into the bodies of humans going through these emotions, I saw energy in motion within them, hearts beating, pumping blood throughout the veins running, connecting to every system in their body. Brains trigger atoms, molecules, electrons, neurons with electromagnetic waves, firing off multiple times per second, sending off messages of anger, hate, annoyance, fear, and the utter intention to destroy what they saw in front of them as they yelled and expressed disease, spreading on to others like wildfire.

The cells in the bodies were depleting at record speed; systems were working on overload and overtime to replenish new blood, new chances for rejuvenation and healing, but the systems were set to default, cycling and reforming cells into disease.

The light in my orb dimmed as I was shown the in-depth truth of human society and the impact it was having on the course of all life. *Forgive them, for they know not what they do.* And with that said, Ezekiel replenished my light again.

Man, where were you when I was having my human experience? I could have used this insight. I finally ringed in with questions.

His light twinkled. I felt giggly. He replied, *I was by your side every step of your journey. When you asked for help, I did what was in my power to do. How much help you were willing to receive in, is on you.*

Again, as he explained, he showed me glimpses of my life that he had his hands in on and times when I wouldn't listen, insisting on my way. *You have to know when to ask for help and get over the ego on default back to humility.*

He showed me back when I was a child asking with intention for help with the demonic figures in my room. As I was watching, I felt the feelings of faith, fear, and openness the child was reacting to. He pointed out, *You see, fear in this case showed up for you to scare you into a position of change. You were the movement for love. Like a teeter-totter, you leaned into love, healing the fearful energy left in that vortex from prior events.*

Ezekiel scrolled through a time line of events taking place in that space like a projection screen recorded and playing out in time. I noticed a familiar boy living in that house. It was the boy I saw walk through the wall in the hallway. He used to live in that house, and everything was coming together now.

That boy lived in a tough world. Beaten daily, proclaimed by his father and uncles of his worthlessness, that he wouldn't amount to anything. While he was in solid form, aberrations of demonic and angelic beings were fighting a battle all around them. The little boy's mother would come in after the beatings and cry with him. It was then that the presence of the angels took over. She prayed for help as she cradled her child, but the boy's light was dimming.

Mother and child were later strangled and beaten to death under the influence of an inebriated mental takeover of his father. Circumstances, patterns, and events all led to my mother and me living in that house at that moment, in the illusion of quantum space and time. A healing was needed there, and we were the ones to follow through with it, and I saw now how it changed the course of not only our lives but with my father's presence no longer being welcome in the space. Life was restored, healed, and light shined for others to pass on for the higher good of us all.

It was all in balance. The concept of time threw the human mind through loops, but seeing the bigger picture realigned in this mathematical grid to new possibilities, for stronger bonds, expanding to new paths and connections.

Knowing that soul taking on human experiences, feeling pain and getting stuck in fixed beliefs, gave purpose to all human souls.

For every scar made, like cells of the body coming to the aid, souls came together with purpose of healing for the higher good of the whole, for us all. We were not alone. Our friends were waiting our requests. It was up to us to feel what we didn't see and finding the courage within ourselves to trust it, to trust all creation.

I leave for you my song. Until next time, I will be helping the other side, who is always on our side.

BLEEDING DRY

If this is as high as I go, I'd rather not
plateau—I'll quit right now for good
In what my life line has to show, what is it that I take
back home? All the while "doing what I should"
There isn't a word for what we are, everything and
nothing, collecting scars—what is the purpose here?
Feeling invisible and under the radar, like a grain of sand
drifting a far—sign of the times is drawing near
Follow your bliss or ignorance is bliss? What is it?
Life is too short, some dreams must wait.
In the end I fold, I hesitate
There was so much with this time I wanted to do.
So set and fixed on my dreams coming true
Nothing is forever with begins and ends, living
heaven and hells, we play pretend
I've gone too far for you to understand the
mysteries of fate is out of my hands
And no one will see it coming when I'm gone.
I'm letting go and yes, life will go on
It's just my luck as the curtain calls me to fly—I'm
stuck on the ground with my words bleeding dry

CHAPTER 5

Mind over Matter

Queens, New York, 1976

The more my parents fought, the more I came to understand why they fought. As the only child to Henry, my father who so badly resented the fact he didn't have a son, and Emma, my mother who resented not only my father's resentment but also the fact that she couldn't have any more children, I understood them by the emotions they projected. Through expressing their un-wanting out on each other, I felt unwanted. I felt as a child that I had no choice but to agree with what I heard my parents saying. How else could I learn anything?

My name is Sonja Parker. I was named after my grandmother from my mom's side who made her way here from Belgium at the beginning of the Second World War. They say I was a miracle due to the complications at birth. According to doctors and my parents, I'm not supposed to be alive. My mother and father were never shy at relaying that to me. In return, I felt that I didn't belong in the picture right from the start.

At the age of ten, I'm now wondering while I am here sitting on the couch, watching *Wonder Woman*, if the fighting will ever stop, and if they didn't want me, then why was I here? I tried to drown it out by turning up the volume on the TV, but it seemed like they would purposely go into the other room and yell louder than the television about all their resentments and regrets, making sure I could hear them.

Were they hoping I would disappear and magically be gone when they came back in the room? Some days I wished for that. That's why I liked to lose myself in *Wonder Woman*. I wanted to be strong, brave, and independent like her. I told myself, *I can make it on my own, I don't need my parents. As soon as I'm old enough, I will move out of here, then maybe we will all be happy.* And so it was, so I thought.

I waited tables through college, got a business management degree at NYU, and opened up my own restaurant at the age of twenty-five, "Sonja's Bistro." Grand opening night, it hit me: if I focused enough on something I wanted, it would happen. I felt like I got what I wanted, but the buried feelings of being unwanted still remained, leaving me unfulfilled. Nevertheless, I had every reason to celebrate that night, and that I did as well.

That night after we closed up the restaurant, my roommates and a few coworkers went out for drinks at a bar in Manhattan. That was where I met the man of my dreams named Nicholas Hill, an investment banker that just landed a job at the World Trade Center, and he wanted me like I wanted him. They say, "When you know, you know," so we jumped right into it and were married the next year. Two years after that, we had our firstborn, Stephen.

Like me, Stephen was named after his grandparent. Nick didn't remember his father. It was reported that his father died a few years after the Vietnam War from Agent Orange. Nicholas was just a baby. He is a very traditional man, so he felt it was a kind gesture to pay tribute to his roots, and I went with his plan.

He was a good dad when he was home. He worked long hours to provide the best lifestyle for the family. The restaurant was also doing well, so we carried on, and I carried two more of his children, Christina and Josh, named after our favorite roommates in college; we never told them that though.

Ten years into our marriage and three kids later, I could feel the resentment building up about Nick being a better father than he was husband. Emotions were coming to the surface that I pushed back down as fast as I could identify them. Suddenly babysitters fell through, and our weekly date night did too. Nick didn't seem to mind the adjustment so long as he could be with the kids, flying kites at central park and even learning how to Rollerblade.

Why did we ever have children? It ruined that moment of bliss, that spark and excitement we had when I fell in love with him. I was starting to feel lack of attention on me that used to fill me up every day. I felt like I should be credited for having his children that he loved spending all his free time with. I went back to the "I don't need them" attitude. I didn't see this coming. All I could think of was that my restaurant was a success, and I could afford to live without them. I cast myself out of the "we" back into "me." *What about me?*

Our bed grew cold. After a long day at work, then coming home and spending time with the kids, Nick was exhausted. Being the owner of a restaurant, it was up to me to make sure everything was still running when someone called in sick or suddenly quit, so I didn't mind staying later and coming home when everyone had already gone to sleep.

The three-bedroom apartment started to feel cramped. As I felt so alone, the joy and love everyone else was sharing and spreading to each other passed by me, even pushing me into a corner, smothered in my own self-doubt. The boys shared a room, and Christina got her own room, which none of them ever bothered to clean up, and Nick never enforced it. He wanted them to have a chance to be kids before rules kicked in. I wanted what they had.

September 11 triggered not only resentment but guilt. I stayed late at the restaurant the night before and slept passed seeing Nick off to work that morning. How was I to know I would never get the chance to see him again, to tell him that I was grateful of how great of a father he was, and that I did want him? More than just words, I wanted to show him and let him feel what was deep down trying to get out.

What was I going to do with three kids under the age of ten? I swore off my parents when I went to college. They'd never even met their grandparents nor were they ever going to if I had anything to do with it.

At that point, I didn't know how to take care of my kids by myself, except by bringing home a paycheck. I did what I had to. Stephen and Christina would ride the bus to the restaurant after school, and I set my office up in the back of the restaurant for Josh's playroom until he was old enough to go to school.

I sold the apartment and bought another in the building above the restaurant so I didn't have to worry about the inconvenience of traveling to and from schools while making a living. Plus, it would be easier for me once they all went off to college and moved out. I just knew that's what they'd do. They loved their father more than me anyway. I felt like by doing the best I could for me would be the best for them. I didn't know how to be any other way.

Every day there was some sort of battle with them—whether it's fighting with me over bedtime, brushing teeth, eating their dinner, doing their homework, cleaning their room, and even watching TV. They ignored me, told me how much they wished their dad was still alive and that it should have been me that died.

Well, I had heard that all my life and thought I was desensitized to the words, but it really just validated how I already felt about myself. I felt shredded apart, like something had been scraping at the cords that had once attached me to my children; they were now severed. We all did our best to not kill each other while we had to live under the same roof. My bucket was empty, and I couldn't fill theirs that they so wanted from me, but I felt I had nothing to give at the time but walls and a roof.

Eventually, the kids did move out, and life went on without them around. Stephen and Christina went off to college, and Josh enlisted in the army straight out of high school. It's fascinating how the feeling of emptiness can somehow get emptier if you focus on it long enough. My bucket seemed to be getting bigger and harder to fill.

I spent more time with Josh than the other two kids. I couldn't afford daycare on my own, so he stayed with me at the restaurant. He was a quiet child and stood in the background, especially around Stephen and Christina, who were constantly competing for their father's attention.

There were also a couple years that it was just the two of us as he was finishing high school. Sure, we didn't talk much, but he would still come down to the restaurant for dinner almost every night and made friends with some of the waitresses. He was a lady's man and had the charm of his father. I felt it was too late for redemption with him. I had already failed as a mother. I was sorry that I never tried with him. I was sorry for a lot of things, but I didn't have time to think about it until I found out I had all the time in the world to and just didn't.

It was at Josh's funeral that I saw Stephen and Christina again. It had been six years since I last saw Stephen and three years when Christina left for college. I should be proud they both got into great schools. Stephen got a football scholarship to the University of Florida. Go, Gators! Christina got accepted in to Vanderbilt University.

It was hard to blame them for wanting to move so far away. I did the same thing when I was that age under different circumstances.

They had flown back to New York, hoping to see their brother, their brother's body, one last time to say goodbye, but instead we were given ashes of his remains and a flag representing his life he gave for the war this world in fighting. They told us that the blast from the bomb made the remains from his body unidentifiable except to the members of his platoon who were there during the explosion.

It was hard for me to believe that my son was dead even sitting in front of the tombstone with his name on it. Was I that horrible to be around that what I thought was my closest son would want to leave me too? It felt like my childhood of nobody wanting me or wanting to be around me. What was wrong with me? Was I unlovable?

I invited Stephen and Christina out for dinner at the restaurant for old time's sake, but they both declined, in a hurry to get back to their lives. I always felt like they were so ungrateful for all I sacrificed for them to get nothing in return…except cancer.

I knew about it before Josh enlisted; I just never said anything to anyone. I knew they wouldn't care anyway. It wouldn't change anything, so why bother?

Lying alone in the hospital, wondering why I got dealt these cards. Had I gotten my *Wonder Woman* wish that I could do it on my own? Was this what I deserved?

The nurse asked if I had any family to call to let them know. *To let them know what?* I thought. That I had a few days to live, maybe a few hours, who knows? I mustered up the energy to shake my head. Even if they did care, my kids had been through enough pain losing their father and brother.

I left this world the same way I entered it, alone.

GO TO THE LIGHT

Where did my soul go? / Set out on this day / A new
tomorrow—there's a better way to shed your sorrow
Into the unknown—to the grand bizarre / Reach out to
the stars from your satellite. Reach out to the light
There is a love / The kind you've always dreamed of—a parallel/ far
away from the hell you've been through. Go to the light—you will
understand / We'll reunite—let the soul expand / Let it be tonight
Does the mind's eye know / The reruns it plays / And how it
swallows—the life you once prayed, you wished would follow?
In silence it's shown—inner avatar/ Under the radar
but not out of sight—come back to the light
Here is a love / The life I've always dreamed of—I must have fell /
To break open the shell to see you go to the light—to the promised
land / Hold on and sit tight—just take my hand / We'll go tonight

CHAPTER 6

Connection over Correction

Sonja... Sonja, I heard calling while I stood staring at a machine with a flat line moving across it. I was in shock as a high-pitched tone notified the doctors of an emergency. It was my lifeless body lying there on the hospital bed that was the emergency. Oh wait, that *was* my body.

Nurses and doctors came rushing in, trying to resuscitate my human remains with no success.

Sonja, I heard a soft voice beyond the loud ringing of the machines and commotion from the hospital staff. Who could be calling my name? I turned to my side, and standing next to me, a glowing mist formed what appeared to be an angel. She was beautiful, smiling softly. She said my name again. *Sonja, it's time to go.*

It took me a moment to come out of shock. Things were still unclear and a little disoriented. Could I still somehow feel the morphine?

It's time to go where? I asked in confusion. *I just got here,* I thought.

Reaching out her hand, so calm and peaceful, *Come with me,* she insisted.

I felt pure love and acceptance radiating from her energy field that rippled into mine immediately. I trusted her completely and openly. It felt like a newborn baby trusts their mother. It just felt right, like the natural next step.

I took a hold of her hand. Instantly a tingling sensation rushed through my body or this figure that looked like my body. It wasn't like a skin touch, but more like my skin had been removed along with bones, muscles, and every other part of my body that had experienced pain or pleasure before. It was like she touched a part of me for the first time, like a light being turned on or the force of energy that carries the wind for birds to soar on, like a wave in the sky.

Then something happened that really took me for a ride in a sense that I couldn't tell if we stood still and the world shifted around us, or was it the other way around?

There was no time travel that my mind had grown accustomed to. It was as if time overlapped itself, infused with all space and creation at once, and we could just flip a switch. We traveled to the funeral set for me.

Although I was never religious, a ceremony had taken place at a small chapel in Queens close to my childhood home. I recognized an elderly couple as my parents sitting in the front row. I felt forgiveness and understanding in my being for my family, feeling like it was all meant to be just as it is; yet my human personality was still present, flowing through my energy field, cycling out toxins. My human thought process was surprised they are still together, but then again, after I grew up and moved away, maybe life got better for them.

Stephen and Christina sat on the other side of the chapel. This would be the first time they were in the same room as their grandparents. I wondered if they would meet each other or just leave like they did at Josh's funeral. *Josh!* I thought out loud. *Why can't I see Josh?*

Besides parents and children still alive were a few coworkers from the restaurant, mingling as though they were using this as an excuse to get together outside of work. I was really surprised that I didn't have all the answers.

Can I see Josh now? I turned to this angelic being beside me for answers.

She spoke softly as though none of my worries mattered to her. *You may see him as soon as you stop thinking about yourself. You will reach that level of consciousness soon enough.*

Thinking about myself? How was this not about me? I must still be in shock. *Are you supposed to be my guardian angel or something?* I asked to find out where this was going.

You can call me Isabelle. I'm a guide. Angels have other realms to work in or a different department, for your understanding.

Whoa! What just happened?

I felt like I blinked, and suddenly we were in my apartment— my cold, dark, and empty apartment. Not empty in the total sense, I had decent furniture and appliances, but in the lifeless sense. Dust accumulated on the windowsills. Isabelle swooshed her hand toward my face, wafting stagnant, stale air at me to bask in.

Is this what you always wanted?

Did I just breathe in humility? I felt my emotional guard drop as though a curtain had just been opened up in front of me. A moment of truth, and yet somehow, I could still feel my stubborn attitude creeping around like vomit.

What is the point of showing me this? Is it to make me feel regret? Well, it's too late for that.

As quick as snapping her fingers, we flashed back into our old apartment. The children were still little, and Nicholas was sitting on the floor in the living room with them coloring.

I felt an urge to reach out to this lingering memory and stuffing it into my pocket for keepsake. We focused on me sitting at the dining-room table, writing out checks for monthly bills. Then Isabelle did this thing, flipping an invisible button; she turned over lenses in my optics to one of the most high-tech thermal cameras I had ever seen. Colors were moving and reforming through our bodies like lava lamps. Mine was perhaps redder than others, but I could also see a vibration of waves flowing out from the crowns of everyone's heads.

Nick's frequency linked up with the children's energy like a synchronized melody playing through the air. My frequency appeared more like an aggravated bubble pushing their beautiful melody away from me.

Okay, I admit I was jealous of the relationship that Nicholas had with the kids. I had never seen such an angry bubble before. I couldn't help but to laugh at myself a little. It has a different feeling, looking back at it this way.

Now we are making progress. Isabelle acknowledged as though she already knew why I was laughing at myself. She continued, *This is the difference between connection of relationships and correction of relationships.*

She switched the grid and zoomed in on the circuits in my brain firing off in a pattern that was literally off the charts of a graph drawn out in such a way to visually see roadblocks being created as brain circuits were rewiring themselves off course of what I felt was once a beautiful scenic road trip turned into a construction nightmare of a detour.

Blood cells were being distributed throughout my body on a mission to set up camp to suck the life from others. It moved in repetition like a pattern designing itself within, declaring the base of "camp cancer" in my liver.

Shaking off the visuals, I was ready to move on to something else.

So I did that, I admitted. *I intoxicated myself through my emotions. I mean, what can I do to make this better?* I asked Isabelle with all sincerity.

Given the chance to change, what would you have done differently? she answered back with a question.

Well, I would have chosen to enjoy this moment. I would go color with them.

Nodding her head, agreeing with my decision, she came back with, *It's easier said than done.*

Indeed, I agreed.

She quickly spun the moments back to my childhood home where I was watching myself alone on the couch, listening to my parents' argument, watching *Wonder Woman* in the background, and again with the thought vibes radiating out of my head and grids of circuits disconnecting and rewiring in my brain.

Something struck me as a different scene happening with the cords triggering in my brain. This was what I would guess a heartbreak looked like to the mind. Wires were snapping in half, spitting out sparks, and desperately reaching out to any other circuit to hold on to aside from the one it just broke away from. It looked like a power line snapped, flopping around like a fish on the ground, spitting out sparks violently.

Although there was an intense energy in the room, I could feel peace of mind, like a light shining in on a tunnel. I could feel it was coming from Isabelle and rubbing off on me. It was a beautiful vibration, connecting love with the innocence of a child. I wondered if Isabelle ever had children, and if so, I would guess that she was a good mother.

My thoughts were interrupted by a dominate energy. *This is when you decided that you were unlovable. This is you deciding to shut off the flow of emotional feelings and manipulating any chances of real connections in life. This is controlling the situation to find the way around the pain. This is the human paradox where the mind is manipulated to believe that by avoiding the pain, the body will grow stronger. Haven't you ever wondered why pain and gain rhyme?*

I stared at her for a moment until I realized it was a serious question. Thinking about it now, I would say that I hadn't thought much about it before. With no filter of verbal communication, I felt vulnerable to the fact that she knew my answer as fast as I was thinking them. I recognized the dominate energy when she spoke telepathically. She had clear intention as her way of communicating.

I began to wonder how she must feel with all my thought, questions, and confusion flying around in these frequencies and vibrations she was showing me. Then I suddenly realized she was waiting patiently for me to stop vomiting the chatter of my mind. I found that locking eyes with her helped bring me back into the moment, a connection perhaps? I'll pat myself on the back for that later. I feel a sense of urgency. Who knows when it's time to move on again?

Isabelle lightened up a bit. I could tell by the look on her face that she had just witnessed that whole thought process in amusement. *Do you remember what we were talking about?*

Then it hit me. In my life, I had never had such an open conversation like this and yet, *No. I don't recall the last thing I heard, that I was open to listening to you about, that I was connecting to the frequency of you when... Oh!* It just clicked back into place. A connection, I did it! We did it!

I lit up with excitement. Again, I felt a sense of urgency to keep moving on. I wanted to stay with this feeling, so I focused back on Isabelle.

No pain, no gain, she reminded me. *By resisting pain or anger only intensified more pain and anger. Whatever you resist persists.*

Another rhyme to remember, I thought, interrupting her shared wisdom again.

She patiently continued, *Disconnecting and reconnecting—all the time you were choosing what to connect to, and you connected very well to pain, discomfort, and anger, creating a cycle of pain throughout the map you insisted on drawing out, rewriting, so you could feel in control of your own pain in that way so you knew exactly how to cope with it by denying it. You denied that you had everything to do with it. You denied your power in cocreating. It wasn't happening to you. You were happening to you. You traveled your own road so much and often that you paved trails that only you allowed navigation through. No one else could get in. You left no room or outlet open to connect with.*

That truth rang strongly within me, so much I could feel vibrations igniting inside my energy field, regenerating a more-attractive energy. I was shifting into another realm of discovery. I had been walking on a path weighing me down and covering me when I could have felt this release of *dis*covering. Ah huh! Another click, another connection made. As this energy was becoming clearer, I noticed the silhouette of Isabelle next to my child self as clear as looking in the mirror.

You were there with me? I asked.

Empowered with the progression of my vision, she smiled and nodded. *I was there every step and thought.*

Suddenly an overwhelming vulnerable feeling took over me. I definitely feel stripped down and naked. Again, she nodded. *Yes, I've seen you naked.* I couldn't help but laugh, embracing the feeling that she knew me better than I might know myself or understand myself. I liked her. I could have used a friendship like this in my life, or rather, I could have used the knowledge of this friendship I had had all along. Isabelle was completely accepting of my screwups, and what some might see as an epic failure in life, she saw love, growth, and connection. Her focus had always been to help me clean up all the debris I collected.

This one connection changed all my other connections. I could feel I still had *dis*covering to connect and *re*solving to correct. With infinity, I knew that that could be done. It was being done through all of us. I'm starting by building new paths in the direction of connection with other frequencies, connecting to people instead of trying to correct people.

I knew better now, knowing that it was an important part of my journey to experience this just the way I did, however it might feel. I had the power and always had it inside me to choose my thoughts and fortify my emotions. I just got distracted and lost looking for something outside of me. Life was such a beautiful gift that I was to understand through contrast.

Isabelle continued to share her light, guiding me to Nicholas and Josh, connecting and shining the combination of light forward. Connecting all these lights, I finally didn't feel alone anymore, not that I ever was.

SOB

(Sonja's on Board)

A rose is a rose. It is what it is. Love is love, and here we are
abused and reused, beating our own drums, dying with every
hit. Like a climax of a song building up to burst. Dispensing
recycled cells, evolving to our highest selves reducing into one.
Living on in memory, reproducing more one of a kind cells,
labyrinths, and fingerprints, connecting to everyone you see.
Visualizing keeps them within, making us one. It's a puzzle
to solve by connecting the imprints in sequence of each
frequency in the consciousness. It's not about forcing heaven
from earth. It's about planting heaven in hell, gathering the
light from a dark place, acting out the scenes, seeing face to
face. Not trying to kill all around you before it can kill you.
Unconscious of the space between, negative ions help us
breath through the night. The light blinds me, taking
me further away from love. What I love is here and now,
not struggling to rise above. Who shines the light on the
darkness, is to say that I'm wrong and make me doubt. But
my roots in the darkness would die if they are forced out.
Beyond my reach of here and now, reaching out to the ones around,
reaching out in the dark. Please take my hand. It's part of the plan.

CHAPTER 7

The Balance

Richard Somerset, or shall I call you Dick?
    Well, I thought, *it depends on the context.*
    I must have fallen asleep because I didn't really know how I got here, standing on the side of a country road, peering out to rolling hills, an open meadow, and a pond…with a car in it filling up with water.
    I felt weightless, a surreal concept of what I was used to. It felt oneness with the sun shining down on me and likewise returning light back mutually. I was the light.
    The paradox of the car crashed into the body of water absorbed my attention. My vision zoomed in like an eagle eye. I was looking at my body, once in the driver's seat, now launched halfway out of the vehicle, tied up in a complex manner between the seat belt and the steering wheel.
    How did I get here? Is this a dream where I blink my way into the middle of the next scene? I heard laughing.
    What a cliché for the mind of a playwright to think in states of scene to scene.
    Turning to my right side, I saw a man, a well-endowed man, visually exquisite to the eyes. This was a tall man with all the physical qualities of human perfection. He had the face structure of a Greek god, muscles of a gladiator, a flawless physique. His gold-plated armor over his nude physical form was like a picture that said a thou-

sand words. Jewels bedazzled all around his armor that screamed, "I am the best of the best!"

I could feel his passionate essence in my core like his energy was instilled within my force field. Beyond the strength radiating from his muscles and chi were giant wings stretching out from his back that, I needed not ask to know, had the power to carry a dragon across the world and back.

Wait a minute! Wings, I thought. *This is not a man, but this is definitely a dream.* He reached out, resting his hand on my shoulder. I was torn if he was doing that out of comfort and sincerity or claiming dominance with his earthshaking power. Maybe there was a little of both.

As I crept out of my insecurity, I locked eyes with this magnificent being; I felt caught in a trance of ocean waters twirling through his alluring eyes. The waves in his eyes were speaking directly to me. *Slow down and focus on one thought at a time.* Surrendering to the trance brought me back into the moment.

Yes, you can call me Dick. I'm used to it, I replied back, trying to catch up to the conversation. *And you are?* I added for my own comfort.

I'll get to who I am later. I will tell you, Dick, that I've looked forward to this for a long time, literally. His face contorted into a mischievous smile as he said "literally." He flipped his hand to the side as though he were controlling the picture I was seeing through a projection screen, scrolling back to another picture.

It was me outside playing in the yard of the home I grew up in. An old English-style stone cottage in New Hampshire much bigger than we needed, but we never went without (that is how I saw it anyway). Surrounded by acres of fields, and there I was at my favorite spot to play under an old oak tree on the side of the red shed.

The shed had a carved roof in the shape of an archway, a perfect structure for me to imagine it as a giant portal for spirits, angels, saints and all beings alike to come and go, especially to come and watch my shows I enjoyed putting on for their entertainment.

As a child, I preferred live theater over the television box. I loved the feeling of connection of real people on stage in front of a real audience, playing out all kinds of stories and scenarios. I still haven't found a feeling as satisfying as that simple moment at the end of a scene when the lights go out, the characters holding their dramatic positions to stretch out that moment for just one more second, uniting all involved in that space and time before they dart off stage and the curtain closes in preparation of the next scene.

My mother, Camilla, would always take me to the theater every chance she could. My older brother, Edmund, followed my father's footsteps as a mason, and neither one of them found entertainment in the arts, so that worked out for me in that way. Sometimes my father would get called down to the big city for new construction jobs on huge, major buildings.

In the summertime, when Edmund and I had a break from school, we would go visit my father in the city. Edmund, in his teen years, took the opportunity to work with my dad to get any extra work experience he could while Mom and I would go see all the Broadway shows.

New York City had certainly grown and changed from the '70s up until now. I remember one trip when Mom and I were walking through Times Square back to our hotel room after a show. She told me about my great-grandmother who used to own a cabaret in an old building inherited by her parents, and that's how she met my great-grandfather.

My mother's side had quite an eclectic array of people and unions while my father's side leaned more toward tradition. Masons and soldiers were a common theme on that side of the family. Stern, hard-working, and a man of few words was how I knew my father to be. Edmund was named after my father, Edward, who was named after his father, and so on.

I, on the other hand, wasn't exactly in the plan. After Edmund was born, my mother miscarried three times, which led them to believe there wasn't going to be any more coming, until I surprised them a decade later. With such an age gap between me and Edmund, I ended up playing by myself most of the time. Well, I wasn't really by myself; I had an audience.

Watching my life fly by so fast, I tried to hold on to those linger-ing memories that brought us back to the oak tree where, as a child, I must have been five years old and performing a Shakespearian mono-logue for my audience of friends that came across galaxies far and wide to join me that day. This was where this big beautiful man/bird insisted that I focused on right now.

Sure, this made sense. I went on to become a very successful screenwriter, if I might say so myself. People had seen my movies all around the world. I gave to charities and tried to be a good man, so what was I seeing this for? What could or should I have done differently?

Wait for it, my male escort requested. Was what I was seeing really happening? I rubbed my eyes to clear my vision to the entrance of the shed. Lo and behold, it was a portal and one that entities, spir-its, and figures of many different shapes, time eras, colored orbs, and auras came flowing out of the portal occupying chairs and blankets that I had set out for them prior to my show.

I knew I wasn't crazy! I shouted with excitement.

He countered back with, *Then how come you let this happen?*

My performance was suddenly interrupted by my father yell-ing from the front porch. "Richie, quit prancing around like a little fairy boy. It's time for dinner!" My father was completely oblivious to the vortex surrounding him like a dusty grey tornado. He looked through it at what he thought was a silly little boy that needed to grow up right away.

Me as a child, of course, heard my father's call and turned back to my audience, declaring an intermission. "Thank you very much! You have been a wonderful audience. Until next time!" the child said, bowing to the crowd as neon colors swirled around him like the northern lights up close and personal.

As I watched myself run toward the front deck, my dad joked in a superior, egotistical tone, "Who are you talking to, boy? There's no one out there." He snickered as he slammed the screen door on his way inside the house.

Why would he say that? Couldn't he see everyone gathering out there in celebration? I as a child opened the screen door followed by

Edmund, who held the door open above my head as I stopped in the doorway to take one more look and wave good night to my friends. They were gone. It was just a shed with empty chairs under an oak tree, and the brightest colors to see was the red, orange, and yellow fall leaves floating away with a gust of wind.

With his free hand, Edmund placed it on my shoulder, leading me inside. "It's okay, Rich. Come on, let's go eat supper." I took a deep breath and sighed, turned, and went inside.

As the door swung shut, slamming into the doorframe, the tip of an ancient sword stabbed the ground near my feet. Realms and dimensions intertwined with a grid system in sync with vibrations rolling like waves in every direction. We followed a wave carried out from the house immediately after the door closed. It rippled out far beyond the earth and, in doing so, disintegrated a number of endangered species. Green flies and Arabian butterflies became instantly extinct.

Horrified to see the reality of such destruction before my eyes, I desperately asked, *What just happened?* The angel pulled his sword out of the ground as if a twisting a lever; the grid system shut off.

That is what happens when instinct gets shut down. That part becomes extinct. You are more than you know. You are more powerful than you think. You have more love in you that you can't even imagine, and then this flipped a switch, stopping atoms from evolving, stopping faith within you from growing, and not just in you. You saw what happened "out there" because of what happened "in here." Tapping on his head, he continued, *In all the possibilities within the quantum physics of your being.*

Even speaking telepathically, I could feel intensity in his voice growing. *If you trusted your instincts, if you held on to what you know to be true to you, what you saw is possible*—pointing to the shed—*the probability of what this would look like now in the realm of all things.*

He stabbed his sword back into the ground, and I became a witness of heaven on earth. All the colors came back in full throttle. Every element as far as my eyes could see were thriving, illuminating, and glowing auras that reached for the skies; plants that had never been heard of, exotic animals, and the tranquil breeze of crisp, clean air surrounded them in such vibrant hues.

While we basked in the exquisite ambience of beauty beyond my wildest imagination, he laid out another grid in front of me. This one looked more like a circular road map, some roads connecting with others, intersection, and some dead ends, more than I'd like to be seeing.

He went on explain that this was my life map. *But your love and faith in love only goes so far now before it gets shut down. You've decided to never marry, that you can't trust anyone to have your children because part of you knows that if this carries on in the same direction, you would be setting them up to fail, and who would want to be accountable for that? If you were to have children, and these fixed beliefs ripple out for generations, here is what we are looking at in less than one hundred years.*

My life map vanished, and as he turned his sword clockwise in the ground, the soil shifted from thriving to depriving, murky, and desolate. What stones were remaining erect from the structure of our home were in ruins. *There is a struggle in your mind. There is a war on earth, and there is a battle going on as we speak in the cosmos.* My jaw dropped with the wisdom of expansion of this physical world as I knew it. A tingling vibration began to shake around me and through my energy field.

This is the goal here. He rotated his sword back counterclockwise to the thriving and tranquil environment of all nature and beast living together in harmony. Even my shoulders relaxed as though tension had died and been released into forgotten memories.

In full agreement, I replied, *Okay, so what can I do now? I'm a dead man.*

His response, *Like an infinite hour glass, it's never too late to turn the sands of time.*

He pulled his sword out from the ground and swooshed his hand to the side, scrolling back to us standing on the side of the road, facing my body lying across the dashboard of my car. Sirens were approaching.

An attractive woman in her late twenties had pulled over to report the car wreck to the police. A few other cars pulled off the road behind her, wanting to be a part of the event as witnesses. This one woman in particular really caught my attention as I watched a wave of colors flowing back and forth from her body to my body, the one lying on the car.

The angel thrust his hand into my chest, the core of my energy field, and jolted me with an energy like a bolt of lightning, rippling out a wave through me to my lifeless body across the field, connecting the wave back to this lovely woman standing beside us, ignoring the waves of energy gliding around her, through her, and right in front of her eyes. The energy continued to float throughout the current of my soul to my body, to her body and energy field as though we were feeding off and thriving from this birth of power cycling within our emotions.

Dick, your mission, should you choose to accept it, is to raise your children in a way that supports their vision.

For clarity purposes, I started to say, *Yeah, but I don't have children.* He leaned his head in to lock eyes with me, to put me back on track of clear intention. Apparently, my eyes dosed off to the wave of energy between me and the woman who appeared to be getting more and more beautiful with every second that passed.

Dick, you are at a crossroads right now. You have a choice. If I send you back to your body, will you choose into love? Will you focus on love, and will you be an example for this next generation of love and accept their vision? With your help and your children's contribution, we can unite heaven and earth. The ripple starts with you.

The ambulance, escorted by multiple police units, arrived to the scene and immediately ran to aid. A sense of duty and honor rushed over me.

Of course, I accept.

I felt a shift in my life map within my consciousness as I opened up; I suddenly knew there was so much more for me to do.

The lights surrounding us were getting brighter, and this angel of a man's smile still shined through it. We turned for a moment, watching the EMTs carry my body from the car onto a stretcher.

He chuckled as he moved his hand to the center of my back as though I were made of matter and said, *Humans are a funny species.*

Sometimes it takes losing lives in order for them to make the best decision for it. One of a kind, no fingerprint alike, no thought process or life map duplicated, no species the same, but man, do we all get a kick out of watching humans grow.

I found myself taken back to my curiosity of who this guy was, if not some kind of human. I asked again, *Who are you?*

As I turned to face him, catching that twinkle in his eye, he winked one eye as he said, *I'll be watching, and remember, there are no accidents.*

With one sudden thrust, he pushed me back, not just off balance but flying into the colorful waves, falling back into my body like two rivers merging into one.

The next thing I remembered was hearing a steady beep of high-pitched tones in the distance. I felt wind passing through my lungs out my nose and cycling around again. Glimpses and quick flashes of where I just came from started fading as my thoughts reached out to here and now. Becoming conscious of my aching physical body, I slowly peeled my eyes open hesitantly to the bright lights over my bed with bars holding me in so I didn't fall out.

I was in a hospital bed with a familiar-looking woman standing over me. I could tell she wasn't a nurse from her fashionable attire. I felt like a child, renewed, focusing on one single thought at a time like I didn't have a choice. Everything was slowed down as though I was working with a blank slate, a clear conscious, and I had some things to learn—like, who was this woman standing before me?

On the same wavelength as my thoughts, I opened my mouth slowly to ask, "Who are you?"

With a sigh of relief and beautifully sincere smile, she said, "My name is Anne. You've been sleeping for three days. I saw your car accident into the lake and just wanted to meet the man that made it out alive."

Like a quick slap to the face, the sight of her standing next to me on the side of the road flashed before my eyes with the words echoing, *Remember, there are no accidents.*

With a blink of my eyes, the vision disappeared. I locked eyes with Anne as a new wave of energy rippled out through us and out into the cosmos.

3 DAYS

Open your eyes to the love that surrounds you. Open your heart
to the light shining through. Free your mind of the past that's
behind you—clear the thoughts of the times you outgrew
Simplify the now in your life with peace of mind—let
imagination come alive. Three days straight, let your soul
thrive—resurrect your heart. God, take the reins and drive
Rational fights to make sense of it all / Practical fights to
be a part of it all. Just like a child, we rise when we fall.
We stand above the waterfall / We fly above it all
In the mind's eye, the mind is set. Are you ready yet to take the
fall in to your heart? / The essence of who you are, has reached
out for days to show you in ways it was never that far away
A child at play / You scar each day when you say "go away." It
has to be my way—for the love of the child inside, stay a while
Maybe all we have is today. Maybe all we have is
three more days—might as well enjoy the stay
Might as well let your inner child play

CHAPTER 8

Born a Slave

"Good morning, Amanda."

I returned back with a smile to Paula, our housekeeper from Cuba, who might be the only warm-blooded person in this drafty house. Okay, maybe my ten-year-old brother, Sam, too. Oh, and our dog, Felix, a well-groomed and mild-tempered golden retriever who was trained like a drill sergeant but by no means stuck up.

My parents, Oliver and Scarlett Roth, expected every one under their roof to be on their best behavior, and that included Paula, who this morning was serving us our traditional breakfast of eggs and bacon with and side of fruit.

"Thank you, Paula," I said as she set the plate down in front of Sam and me.

"Thank you, Paula," Sam echoed.

My father was too busy with his face behind the morning news-paper to acknowledge Paula as she brought in his dish of food.

Growing up in the Hamptons wasn't all it's cracked up to be. All the glitz and glamour of the rich and famous was just show-off to the media's eyes. They see what they want to see. What I see?

Well, I saw my mom on the phone, pacing around the oversized island in the kitchen that she never had made use of except for a cen-ter piece of material to walk around as though it helped the progress of communication over the phone.

My mother was a senator, and all she talked about was who liked who, who was voting for what, and who was backstabbing who.

She sounded like all the stuck-up, rich bitches at my school that didn't know any better than to think that they were better than everyone else because they were raised to believe it. I was told that a private school was best for me so that I could be with others who were more like me. Meaning, born of rich privileges and self-entitled beliefs.

I knew a part of me was fighting this lifestyle, but looking at my parents and how they lived their lives showed me how I didn't want to be. I wanted to be happy.

My father still hadn't put down his newspaper, but he did take a moment to yell at Sam for feeding Felix bacon under the table. The dog was no exception to discipline either.

I couldn't understand how my parents got along. They were hardly ever in the same room. With my father's partnership at one of the biggest law firms in New York, we barely saw him; and when we did, he was usually yelling at us for doing something wrong.

I also couldn't understand how Paula could manage to keep her chin up standing in the corner on the side of the archway in between the kitchen and dining room, watching and waiting for us to eat in front of her so that she could clean up after we're done. Or how that she still stood, posed with dignity, after my father just referred to her as "the maid."

I always admired Paula for her strength, patience, and self-esteem. She brought her family all the way up from Cuba on a boat and fought for citizenship. For what? To be treated like this? I wondered how it was worse for her in Cuba to want to leave and be putting up with this. I knew she must have had good reason, but she still deserved better than that kind of treatment.

After breakfast, Sam and I went into the family room with Felix. Sam got out his remote-control car. He always got a good laugh at Felix chasing it around the room, and we got away with it when it was only us and Paula home, but this day happened to be picture day for our annual Christmas cards.

We were already in our Sunday's best when my mother put down her phone for a moment to lead the photographer into the room. She snapped at the dog for playing, picked up Sam's car that just ran into her foot, and gave it to Paula along with a look of "how could you let this happen?" Sam handed the remote to Paula before he got scolded for it and stood by as the photographer set up in front of the floor-to-ceiling stone fireplace. Yes, we were a cliché.

As my father walked into the room, I moved to the opposite corner with Felix sitting at my feet, but still anxiously directed toward my father. The room always felt dense and heavy when my parents were here; it felt cold. I remember a distinct difference of energy when my parents were home and when it was just Paula looking after us. She brought warmth somehow.

Glancing at this room like a fly on the wall was some extra activity that no one was aware of. Well, maybe Paula and Felix, but Paula seemed like she was always in her own world inside a happy, perfect bubble that no human arrogance could penetrate, and it showed. Invisible to the human eye in this room was the light and darkness filling the area. Beyond the humans, furniture, material matter, and last but not least, Felix, was so much more.

Angels and fairylike creatures surrounded Paula, nurturing her with light that she paid forward, directing it to Sam, Felix, and Amanda. No offense to the photographer, she was just very much aware of her love she had for those innocent beings. As a current of light drifted through the room like glittering dust particles gifting the children with warmth, it, too, enhanced the essence of Amanda and Sam's energy like a protection, locking into spirit guides' and ancestors' vibrations that were also standing near the children, watching over them.

On the contrary was a shadowy force drawing out vitality from the kids, like energy vampires feeding off the negative, selfish, and toxic energy that saturated the air in the room when the kids were confronted by their own parents. The lack of love and connection made for contradicting feelings in the space, like a light flickering on and off.

We never knew when the press or reporters were watching us. Whenever a stranger such as a photographer came into our house, we put on the show of the picture-perfect family, or so the picture projected.

Immediately after the photo was taken of us posed in front of our expensive and meaningless decor on the mantel, my father dismissed the dog outside. It seemed like he only allowed the dog to live with us so he could appear to be humane. I couldn't remember the last time either one of my parents tucked me in or kissed me good night. As long as I was getting a 4.0 GPA (or higher) and won first place and all the accolades I could, I could avoid being yelled at for not doing it good enough and not being like them.

When I was sixteen, Felix passed away. Well, they had Paula take him to the vet to be put down because he was getting too slow. By the time I got back from school that same day, they had replaced Felix with a poodle. Sam and I weren't allowed any emotion or talk of Felix. Feelings made our parents uncomfortable, so that was out of the question. "Suck it up. It's just a dog," they would say, which clearly meant to me, stuff any emotions that try to come up, and relationships were easily disposable. We learned to shut down feelings fast to avoid any extra put-downs for our weaknesses. Meekness was interpreted as weakness; empathy and vulnerability also a weakness.

My junior year of high school opened a door for me that finally gave me the sense of freedom. I started dating Quinn Stuart, who was sure to follow in his father's footsteps into med school. He being a senior had his foot already in the door to some major college parties.

On the weekends, I would lie my way into going to a friend's house to work on a school project while Quinn and I would hit up the parties. Drugs were easier to get than an alcohol, so I stocked up on as much as I could to get me through the rest of the school week. My favorite was anything I could get my hands on or anything I could get a lot of.

Quinn went back and forth from letting go by doing what he wanted and then falling back into the exception of his father. We were also on and off, depending on his bipolar ex-girlfriend Jessica's mood and persistence.

Jessica was a stuck-up beauty queen, and she was a much better suit for Quinn than I was, in his dad's opinion. Quinn didn't care much either way, as long as he had a place to put his dick in. To make his decision easier, I ignored his calls, and eventually he got the message.

My senior year of high school was hazy. I got through my classes and made my grades just like I was used to. Any extra time I had I would find a way to get high. I loved how it made me feel different. I loved that it made me feel good. I could let go and lose myself in whatever it was. Pills were the easiest to hide. They didn't smell, and it didn't take much to do the job. Pop it in, and ta-da! Let the good times roll.

In the early spring, my parents were all over me about college, which ones I applied to, which ones I "should" apply to. Every day they would check in to see if I got any acceptance letters while all the while I was just waiting for their acceptance. Hell, at this point, I would take it in the form of a letter.

Then it seemed like all the acceptance letters came in all at once. That started arguments on which one was best for me, and my parents had a difference of opinions on that while mine didn't matter.

Sam stood by, watching what he had to look forward to, holding the dog for comfort, which I'm glad someone took to and gave attention.

One day, after a rough day at school, I made a few calls, and a friend had a hookup for some Oxis. So two friends and I took a walk to meet up with some guy. Fixated on getting high, my focus was on everyone else's problems. I didn't have a problem with addiction or anything. Getting high was the solution to me.

Making our way down the sidewalk, a homeless man leaning against a building with his hand around his dog, snuggling under a raggedy old blanket, my friends took this moment to look up from their phones to make fun of him and his mutt before sticking their faces back into their cellular devices. Just as I started thinking of how embarrassed I was to be associated with them, a car slammed into a man walking across the street.

The man tumbled over the hood of the car as the driver looked up to see him. Fortunately, not fatal, but unfortunate that when the man picked himself up from the road, he saw the driver putting down his phone on the passenger's seat of the car before he got out to see if the man was okay. Commotion flared up, and a fight broke out between the driver and pedestrian as witnesses ironically took out, or should I say, aimed the phones they already had out to record the fight.

In the midst of the small rioting down the block, we turned down an alley and made the deal.

When we got close to my house, we divided up the pills and went our separate ways. I was in a hurry to get back to my room. More than anything, I needed a release.

After dinner, I was excused to go to my bedroom. I said good night to everyone as I intended on staying in there for the rest of the evening. Simmon, Sam's little dog he named after Richard Simmons because of his tight curls, chased me upstairs, whining. He never did that before. I hardly bonded with him, unlike Sam. Following me all the way to my door for what I thought was a desperate cry for attention, Sam called for him. I leaned down to pet him before I shut my door to my room, leaving Simmon out in the hallway, weeping.

Immediately I grabbed the Oxis out from my pocket and took a few. I didn't think about the dose; I knew I just wanted more. I wanted to feel more and wanted to feel so good I forgot about today and yesterday and all the bullshit in my life.

I turned on some music and lied down on my bed, waiting for the pleasure of the pills to kick in. While I was staring at my ceiling, I began to wonder why my parents were the way they were. Was it for me to be a stronger person? Was love and affection a weakness? Or did they need to be that way so that they could be good at their jobs? Maybe their jobs made them that way.

As soon as I realized my thoughts were running in circles, I started to see tracers on the ceiling. The crown molding looked like it was blowing bubbles out at me. Here it came. I was going for a ride this time. My heart was pounding quickly like an uncontrollable panic attack, beating so fast I couldn't keep up with it. Dizziness merged into a light-headed daze that made the tracers and bubbles circle around me forming a cocoon, closing in on me.

My vision zoomed in and out of darkness like being pushed and pulled in and out of a tunnel. Knowing that this must be an effect from the pills, I surrendered to this new high taking over my entire body. This was what I asked for. I felt a useless game of tug of war that I didn't have the physical strength to play anymore. I was growing tired quickly and shutting down, so I closed my eyes.

In an empty darkness, I felt a presence enter my room, darker than black, like a shadow in the darkness if you could imagine. I could feel one more tug, and suddenly the presence pulled me out of myself.

CONFESSIONS OF AN ADDICT

To love me is to forgive me/ I know not what I do. You
think you don't know me / I was in the dark too.
Behind the shadows you watch in the cave / The lies believed
are not here to save you on the merry-go-round of demons
riding the wave of the thoughts circling around your head.
"I'm better off dead," they scream and shout. It's making me
stronger the longer I doubt myself / I don't see the way out.
Too ashamed to admit I'm addicted to this feeling I've been
dealing with so long. Too ashamed to admit I am wrong,
and this ceiling's closing in, repeating the same song.
Forgive this lonely part of me left in the dark / Thinking reflections
are projections coming from my heart—watching the shadows I
mimic the wall like a slave. The lies I believe have only depraved
me of light I found as I turned around words that I said, so curious
how they got in / Feeling brave, I left the cave / Voices still calling
me in. For the love of me, I forgive me for when I go back again.

CHAPTER 9

Atoms and Evolution

My feet felt like they were weighed down or perhaps linked to rails by a magnetic force securing me to the earth. I had never felt so in touch with gravity before now.

It was pitch black in here. Was I blind? Wait, what was the last thing I remembered? It smelled wet, like a damp cave. In fact, I heard the sound of water dripping like a broken faucet. I was not sure if my eyes were open or shut. Could someone turn the lights on, please?

Instantly a giant spotlight flashed on me more blinding than the dark. I held up my hand to shield the light from my eyes, revealing only a shadow. I rotated my hand back and forth, front side and back side. Call me crazy, I remembered Peter Pan trying to catch his shadow, but how was I the shadow? This felt like a dream where everything weird was accepted as the norm. I felt open to everything and anything possible.

This must be the hangover from the drugs. It felt like the hangover I had coming off anesthesia when I got my stomach scoped for ulcers last year. I feel beyond confused and even more so stuck in the question of, if I'm the shadow, then where was my body? It must be looking for me like Peter Pan.

Giggling echoed, ricocheting throughout the walls of the caves.

Hello? I said hesitantly.

Shh. We have time, I heard them whispered. *She thinks she is still alive.*

Again, echoing through the cave.

Where am I? I asked, hoping I would hear me to know where I could find me. My thoughts circled, but I didn't have a voice like I had been used to. My emotions and feelings carried through the walls as form of communication, but who was listening?

The giggles progressed to loud chuckles.

Shh. Give her a moment to focus, I heard a man say, who didn't seem to be contributing to the laughter. *Just calm down. You need to be present.* For some reason, the laughter was contagious like watching someone playing, enjoying the moment, sucking anyone in to their enthusiasm for life. It might have been dark, but it felt far from scary. I felt safe.

Present, I thought. Okay, let me catch up… I was in my room, passed out, and that's when someone pulled me down and dragged me out. Oh, I remembered. My sight began to adjust to the darkness beyond the blinding spotlight shining down on me like I was being interrogated.

I was in a cave. I put down the shadow of my hand from the beam of light, and there standing in front of me was a tall man in black, all black actually. I couldn't see features on his face, only glowing cutouts for eyes. I could see the outline of a long trench coat and a bowler hat.

Stepping out from behind him were two dark figures to his right and left sides. They appeared more like sketched-out holograms of shadows that maybe once had a body, or dark ghosts drawn by a young child that definitely colored outside the lines. Either I wasn't quite as present as I needed to be or they weren't.

The energy field holding their bodily structures together had a glitch-like static on an old TV. Nerves started to shake in my core like I as having my own earthquake. Faded memories were coming to the surface of me as a baby lying in my crib, watching a merry-go-round of stars twirling above me on the ceiling from a night-light globe on the dresser nearby.

These men came into my bedroom and frightened me to my core, adding on emotions to my human consciousness, giving me new emotions to identify with for my human growth. I felt the same

emotions trembling in front of them now with the wisdom to deci-
pher what's real.

Who are you? Shaking, coming down off the shock, that's all that
came out of me. Still disoriented, I could have slurred my thought
process, so I sat back, feeling that the ball was in their court now.

The tall man in the bowler hat was the only one to speak. The
two behind him only made gestures of emotions as though they were
posing as reserve tanks that he channels through. *You call me Pharaoh,
the archangel of the underground. I represent the energy of dark emotions
and process those emotions back to the light. You will be communicating
to me on this side.*

Now I'm feeling present and giving him my undivided attention. *What side is this, exactly? Where am I?* He dispersed the light
around the cave. Under the impression that we were having a private
conversation, I stood corrected as I saw green glowing figures moving
through the cave systematically, some being guided and redirected by
other distinctive figures as though they had been mining this place
for centuries.

I wasn't sure if my nerves started to calm down or adapted. I
felt a deep encouragement to rise to the occasion. Imagine growing
accustomed to a constant anxiety attack, the complete opposite of
overwhelming excitement of the unknown and determined that the
show must go on. I felt in tune with his energy, consciously knowing
that this was the norm down here. I could feel tree roots stretching,
pushing blindly through darkness, and solid ground connected to its
own limbs being shaken by a strong wind that vibrated back down to
its core. Vibrations were the form of communication.

*It's been referred to as the underground, the origin, your roots,
trenches, and for human's religious purposes by creation of fear, hell.
Since there is no such thing as a hell in the afterlife, only earthbound
spirits held down by G forces. For your purpose, we will call it the origin,*
Pharaoh said.

I have a purpose here? I asked openly.

Although I could sense this man had the confidence of Tarzan
in the jungle, I felt he was taken back.

That's what you got out of what I just told you? He seemed amused.

Since I already decided that I was dreaming, I was all in for the ride. Plus, if he was going to kill me, I think he would have by now. This whole experience amazed me that I could feel his undeniably powerful energy, somehow knowing that he could speak all languages known to man, and surprisingly feel a sense of humor compatible with mine. I mean, this guy was far more powerful than the president; he could be king of the underground, and yet he was being kind to me, telling me that I had purpose. Again, he had my attention.

As I was saying, you will be communicating with me. I report directly to Osiris, Pharaoh explained.

Where do I know that name? I must have thought out loud because Pharaoh answered back.

It is residual cloudiness from the connection you are still holding onto of your human body. The overdose of chemicals in your body stimulated all seven chakras in your vortex to open and unlock the seven ethereal gates, connecting the portals to the seven planets in our solar system. You lit up outer space tonight, Amanda. You just changed the world and will change it even more now that you are here.

Set to be graduating at the top of my class, I knew better than that.

But there are eight planets in our solar system, I remarked.

Again, that's what you got out of what I just told you?

I shrugged. *What about the new planet orbiting in our solar system?* I also cared to mention. It was all fascinating to me. I just wanted to be on the same page.

That's not the point. He continued, *You are born unto the earth, of the earth. Just consider yourself the earth, so this planet cancels out from your equation, but still connected to the other planets in our solar system.*

Okay, I get it. I didn't want him to feel like I was being insubordinate. It's just that he felt like a friend; something was familiar about him that comforted me more than my stone-cold, earthly parents.

You've gotten rusty, Amanda. By the way, I'm going to call you Mandkhora from now on.

As he looked up to the ceiling of the cave as though it were speaking to him, I realized that Mandkhora refers to man-eater. Now how would I know that?

Just like I felt pulled out of my bedroom, Pharaoh, his two companions, and I briskly floated up to the surface of the earth. As we quickly ascended through the earth's layers, they revealed ancient artifacts, fossils, covered ruins, burial grounds, and even a giant colony of ants. I could feel the stored energy as we passed each layer to the top arriving at an Indian reservation.

Oh, that's right. I was Pocahontas in a past life. I could see a colorful ray of light projecting from my energy field equally flowing into Pharaoh's companions, finding humor in my sarcasm. In a serious manner, Pharaoh raised his right hand, cutting off the energy flow, and pushed the current outward, flowing it away from us like he was feeding the earth our humorous vibes.

It was in the middle of the night, and projecting a psychedelic wave of particles would normally draw a lot of attention; this felt like a different realm though, an invisible realm contrasting dark in the dark I could easily hide in the shadows.

Do you see it now? he asked.

What am I looking for? I thought as Pharaoh continued, *Focus. Be here now.* I grounded myself in the present moment with all around me. I felt Pharaoh feeding me thoughts on the position of dualities, the paradox of the lightness in this dark situation that is all one. My vision started clearing up. *In order to attract the most sunlight, one would wear black.* Yes, I agreed. *To be what I am not, I can see who I am.*

Suddenly it hit me. *There it is.* I recognized this place. Again, vibrations were shaking from my core. Something was surfacing. Looking around, I could see clear in the night as fast as I could think it; a lens flipped over my vision like night goggles. In the distance, I saw Mount Rushmore intertwined with a silhouette of the mountain before it was carved out. Even closer, I saw wanderers, earth-bound spirits. I saw history in reality.

Déjà vu hit me into a deeper realization coming to the surface and out. I lived here, and my family was here. It felt like a part of me had been disconnected, like healthy blood and diseased blood running through my veins, and with all seven chakras open, I felt like I could sniff out my own blood like a dog. These were my people, my ancestors, my roots and origin.

A recap played out in front of me. A whole village of Sioux Indians set up, living in peace, building more huts for the growing community of the sixteenth century. Hierarchy was a common theme in my bloodline, and this was no exception. Generations survived the plague that obliterated the vast majority of the world's population for reasons still making its way to the surface through another life.

As a wife of the chief, I had the honor and responsibility to serve our village in any way I could; but as history had shown us by repeating itself, the government wanted control over the land, raiding the village unexpectedly. We could have made it out alive if they had just torched our huts, but to add insult, most of us were shot down, slaved, or locked up. Very few got away, leaving children behind.

The human souls of the ancestors still remained wandering the grounds. I had an overwhelming sense of love for all of them. I passionately wanted them to be in this love with me. They deserved it as everyone did.

The wisdom of past lives connected with me, and I had some business to attend to. This being a different time era and different circumstance, I wondered why my job was here and not back with my family at the present time in the Hamptons.

Pharaoh explained, *The effects of your overdose turned the cycle around for your family at the present time, and together we are closing the gap. What this world doesn't realize yet is that we are all on the same team, the light, the dark, the dead, the living. Even the plague, wars, and numerous events that dropped the human population suddenly and dramatically, to the judgment of the human mind being a tragedy, has a positive side to it as giving us another shot at doing better the next time around.*

I recognized that as numerous other past lives came to the surface and all the wisdom of my ancestors that paved the way to and through multiple lives in multiple spaces in time. We were there for each other in all our other lives in different manners to learn different lessons to ascend to a higher power. Everyone was my brother and sister; we were one big, very big, family.

You will be called to help your earth parents, but like you, they have their own purpose, and as their course is running, now they will be there for Sam. They have shifted their focus more on relationships and less on careers with status quo after the impact of your overdose. They will be starting up a charity to help other families who have also been affected by such losses to come together and support each other.

I could see the whole process happening like future memories as he explained it to me. I knew they would be okay, with all my experience in past lives all coming together now. All wounds must be healed, and family was there, or shall I say "here," for us all to assist in the healing process. As we healed ourselves, we healed our family as a whole. I could project energy to them and receive it from them in a different sense than physical touch. We were still and always would be connected just as everything in the universe was.

Let me show something to you before we get to your new purpose. In the blink of an eye, we shuttled to Central Park. Traveling and projecting through space and time was easier if you had been there some time in the physical form, so this was an easy one for me.

Although it was still dark, we tapped into the energy processing earlier on that day. It was sunny that afternoon with the typical, highly populated activities combined with tourists exploring the scenery. He particularly wanted to focus on the children playing. Energy currents were flowing in and out of the earth's surface. The solid ground turned transparent, revealing the roots under the trees in the same pattern underground as it was reaching for the sky, forming the branches like a mirror. As above, so below; and as there was darkness in the balance for the trees to grown, there was also something else I noticed.

We watched the children playing, toddlers walking, falling down and getting back up, and learning from trial and error. What was happening beyond the human eyes was the energy being recycled to, through, and back up from the earth. When a child fell onto the ground, it triggers an emotion. Since the ground was in the way of the direction the children were failing or falling, the energy of failure kept going in that direction, falling into the earth, turning to black matter, the natural element of the earth; like the human body automatically going to work to heal broken bones, cuts, and even bruised egos, the earth goes through the same process.

Pharaoh showed me that when a child fell down, they released that weakness to the earth, and when they embraced the determination to get back up and try again, they were renewed with a burst of light. The humans stood as mediums for the cycle to flow through. We were the connection to the light and the dark. Through consciousness, thoughts, experience, travels, and most importantly, connections through other physical relationships, we expanded portals throughout the universe.

Now getting back to your purpose, Pharaoh expressed telepathically. We blinked back to the Indian reservation. Pointing to Mount Rushmore, he said, *That is your loophole that will take you straight to me, and from there, I will escort anyone you bring through to Osiris, who will release them into their higher realm. There's no wrong or right way of doing this. It's up to you to find the best way to get them out from their loop or cycle to keep the flow moving and clear out residual energy like a vessel. But there is a sense of urgency. There will be a new wave flushing out the old and in with the new. The angels are moving and regrouping.*

I could sense what I had to do; like coming up to a bridge, my instincts knew to cross it and keep moving forward, but I couldn't see the future as far as he could see it.

So if I can shuttle my family through, do I still have another human life to live?

The sun would be coming up soon. Like a vampire, Pharaoh wanted to get back to the underground as soon as possible. He did his best to prepare me, and I could feel him replenishing my energy as he spoke. His two companions behind him on both sides weren't as subtle as he was with their emotions. They reacted to all the emotions around as fast as breathing and releasing air circulated in the atmosphere.

He went on to explain, *You are the ambassador for the new world, gathering the twelve tribes.*

Wow! That sounds important, I thought. *It's like the more lives I take on, the higher the ranking I go.* I continued listening.

It's like a sock drawer. The drawer itself is one container. Inside it holds not only many socks but different kinds of socks that have been on different journeys and have different connections to other socks in the drawer. Your mission is to usher in the rest of the twelve tribes through our family bloodline. With the seven portals open, you can channel your ancestors from most recent Native Americans clear back to their lineage of ancient Egypt. I recommend starting with your immediate bloodline, and their connections will expand portals. Remember, you communicate to me. Trust in your power. You are the one swinging the pendulum. If you don't lead them all the way to me, they will get stuck in the cell loop, and you will take on that energy in your next human experience. Follow through, Mandkhora.

I knew the sun was coming up, and he was going to the underground, the origin, until I saw him again, but I lingered while I had the company.

So my job is to gather up some socks? I knew I wasn't getting a hug, so I just threw that out there.

Pharaoh's companions expressed the humor for him as he fortified his emotions, answering back. *Every thought is a prayer. Be conscious. Own your mind and seize the day.* And with a fist pump, he and his two companions descended back down into the origin.

I felt the moment Pharaoh and his small entourage hit the underground when the earth's surface rumbled beneath me. Taking flight toward the celestial bodies in all direction was the fastest-growing burst of light projecting into the sky like a nuclear blast. An equal reaction returned back into the atmosphere, bringing with it colossal storms scattered throughout the northern hemisphere of the globe.

The winds began to roll through wheat fields and sagebrush around me without affecting a hair on my vital force. Clouds were forming quickly from the west as a lightning storm moved in. I looked up at the full moon before my vision was to become foggy by this weather event. Reaching out to the satellite, it became clear of what I was walking into.

From a lunar point of view, the structure of the planet formed into a replica of a human brain. Igniting like fireworks, neurotransmitters sparked in the frontal cortex. Old cells circulating in repetition throughout the unit were dying off at rapid speeds and in large groups creating room for reformed, enhanced cells to rush in and take their place for the reconstruction of the whole.

The shift was in motion. At this rate, the human race would be on the endangered-species list, on a universal scale, within the next decade. And so my job began as a human-soul trafficker for the Underground Railroad.

A WAY THROUGH

At the end of the line—the final destination
Caught in the tiger's eye—no time for consideration
Out of desperation—I'm falling back in line
Angled my way from point A to who I came to be
Drawing lines through the circles of life—
still brings me back to you
Burning bridges and chased by time
Strayed from my point of view—I found a way through
A hard journey ahead—I gave up frustration
The best is yet to come—with full on intention
A working progression—centered on what's ahead
Tough enough to take the pain in return of what's to gain
Igniting this voice of silence shining on the darkness
The stillness inside us will find its way through
Opening doors we've never seen before
Connecting me to you

CHAPTER 10

Martial Artist or Partial Artist

In my experience and through the core of my being, I believed in a power higher than myself. In my fifty-three years, I have had my fair share of training, coaches, sensei, and even what some considered to be human angels that sponsored me through AA that led me to my own position of power.

As long as I could remember, I've had a resistance to the mainstream ways of society. Instead of trying out for a typical sports team in high school, I decided to use my natural athletic abilities learning karate. I found that that was the best way for me to manage my teenage testosterone. Plus, two of the highest principles in martial arts were respect and discipline, and that was the perfect encouragement for my parents to climb on board, fully supporting me on that journey.

I'll admit, it was not easy earning a black belt; but then again, if it were easy, then everyone would be a black belt. I learned a lot about myself during my training. For one, it's more than physical skill. Beyond the patience of repetition were mental strength and personal obstacles to break through. A balance of body, mind, and spirit, and the biggest challenge to get in the way was myself. I say this because I almost quit several times throughout different stages of my training, which now I realized were the times I hit walls mentally, allowing that to discourage me; and because of all those moments was why I believed in higher power or powers.

If there wasn't, why would I continue to pick myself back up and try again? Who was seeing through my mind's eye envisioning me as a black belt because I could see me as one? How would I have become a third-degree black belt if there weren't others who earned their rankings before me in order to teach me? My big question, who or what was behind the power of persistence pushing me to continue on with all I have got, one more time, one more kick, one more step? I could always feel a presence of inspiration whispering to me, and I'm glad I listened.

By the age of thirty, I had opened my own dojo in Orange County, California; and by forty, I was celebrating my third degree alongside my third school opening up. With dozens of worthy and respected black belts under my wing, the growth of the martial arts schools was running smooth so that I could expand and express my passion as a stunt double in the Hollywood film industry. I had been fortunate enough to be in over a dozen action films as a double and martial arts choreographer.

When it came to careers and finances, I give myself a pat on the back. Before I lose myself in righteousness, I'm checking my ego as I ponder the reasons why I'm driving to my vacation cabin in the secluded mountains of Colorado for some much-needed R & R. It's just me, Dominic Bridger, and Stella, my fifteen-year-old black lab who has proven to me that soul mates weren't necessarily romantic relationships.

I didn't make kids a priority in my life and had two failed marriages, one of which I got custody of Stella after an argument where I admitted out loud that I trusted Stella more than my now ex-wife, and justifiably so, as both marriages ended due to affairs, not on my part.

I'm not the one to play the victim game and point fingers. I'm accountable for my part in all of it. I was dedicated to my work, my passion for martial arts, expanding my wisdom, and satisfaction in achieving my goals. If I would have put in half of the energy toward my spouses as I did for martial arts, it would have been a different story; but marriage didn't make the cut on my priority list, so I'm not all surprised.

I had folded down the back seats in the SUV so that Stella had a comfortable bed for the road trip and room to stretch her legs if she had the energy to do so. She has had fifteen good years. They were good to me, anyway. I could only pray I gave her a happy, fulfilling life in return. I could tell she had been achy and slowing down dramatically this last year, so she definitely deserved some R & R as well.

Heading east up through a mountain pass, the sun setting behind us was directly aimed straight ahead, illuminating the road, contrasting dramatic shadows beyond the trees lining the street as far as the eyes could see. Like a deer in the headlights, I got caught up in the serenity and beauty of the country. I set the cruise control and mental auto pilot as I began to pray.

Lining both sides of the road, glistening from the warmth of the sun, were angels along with generations of canines from Stella's bloodline, standing by like soldiers honoring their own, clearing the way for safe passage. In the distance, luring behind the angels in the shadows of the trees were dark entities outnumbered and outpowered. As my prayers continued to flow, the number of angels showed up, expanding the light of the sun shining down the path.

The cabin was nestled in evergreens with a beautiful lake view from the front deck. It's no off-the-grid cabin but also not a state-of-the-art modern one either. I called it my Goldie Locks Retreat because it's the perfect balance of old school and amenities. The woodburning fireplace made for a perfect night for me and Stella to cozy up and let go of the rest of the world.

Letting go indeed, Stella passed on in her sleep that night. When I woke up to her lifeless body, I fell into a mental instability that I hadn't felt in a long time. I could honestly say I didn't feel this way in either one of my divorces. It's a funny thing with marriages in the world nowadays—they don't last.

Statistically, one out of every ten thousand people who start training in martial arts will ever earn their black belt. The instant gratification and self-entitled mentality of society has grown rapidly, and coincidently, long-lasting marriages are becoming just as rare as committing to go the distance to achieve a black belt.

Human connections have been severed or disconnected, but Stella had her priorities straight. She knew how to live, how to treat others. Stella reminded me to enjoy the simple pleasures in life and to not take myself too seriously. She jumped through the snow like a deer every chance she could get. She snuggled up on the couch, listening to my days. She relieved my stresses without a word, simply by her presence and her tail wagging wildly every time I walked through the door. Love and companionship were all she asked for, and she returned that tenfold. My love was enough for her, and that made for a long-lasting relationship that we shared. I needed Stella. I needed her example of selflessness.

Achieving my goals as a martial artist was empty if I couldn't share it with Stella. I was praying, speaking to her, as I buried her body on the side of the cabin. I sought out the best view of the lake on the side of the porch where I sat on a rocking chair, staring out to the calm waters. Dazing off, feeling this empty space in my heart, it took a while to realize it was too calm, if there was such a thing. It was like the calm before the storm, even though I just felt like I just went through an emotional storm losing Stella.

While sitting out on the deck, imagining that Stella was sitting next to me, excruciating pains began to run up my left arm. I had felt random sparks of pain for a few days now but thought nothing of it, even considering I was a senior in athlete's standards.

Suddenly it felt like I had been punched in the chest. This was definitely bigger than any broken bones or injuries I had ever sustained before. It took every ounce of strength and energy I had to pick myself up from the rocking chair. With no neighbors close enough to walk to or cell-phone service, I realized I had nowhere to go and no one to call for help.

I heard that inner power or higher source softly say, *Don't fight it, Dominic. Stay calm and let go.*

I had been teaching students that staying calm in self-defense situations was the first thing to remember, and hearing my own words echoed back to me made me feel that there was a reason for everything. Every moment of my life led me to this moment, and somehow, I got to find that trust within myself to walk the talk, to be what I had been taught and had continued to carry on through my teachings.

The shock of the pain stabbing at my chest released as I surrendered to that moment. The last thing I felt was my body hitting the porch in front of the door. Immediately I bounced back up, painless, and there was Stella wagging her tail once again, happy to welcome me home.

"Stella! Oh, Thank you, God!"

Dominic Bridger! A rumbling vibration from every direction shook my vision of the cabin, lake, and mountains. The whole scene was melting away; the earth fell as I ascended to the most glorious kingdom in the skies, a paradise no human could imagine possible, and there I stood before a throne on high.

Lining the floating staircase in front of me were angels ascending up to archangels that were closest to the top of the stairs, blazing a tune of triumph through their trumpets, accompanied by a symphony of angelic voices circling me by the thousands, encompassing me and Stella in such a loving manner that would make any being feel overcome.

I held my head high, peering out to all the celestial beings around me—all of which resembled friends and family of all ages. All these beings were connected to my life in one form or another. I recognized some as my earth brothers and sisters, mother and father, grandparents, students who I taught, exes as archangels and spirits of power in the celestial realm of Valhalla, my heaven.

I shared the wisdom of everyone around me, and I took it all in as they sent me praises, connecting their light with mine. These souls still had connections to human bodies remaining on Earth as their soul remained free to be here with me to share this moment as their higher selves wrapped in the finest robes, illuminating auras that could stun the cosmos. Even Stella was dressed for the occasion in a most-desirable golden robe. This was a moment of *awe!*

I knelt at the bottom of the stairs before the man on the throne of whom I am ascending to become as he presented me with a pair of superhuman feathered wings, brilliantly white with golden highlights, and a ravishing scepter. On it a shifting array of lights covered by an impenetrable orb, like a giant, glittering Christmas party in a crystal ball. I felt a thundering power jolted into me as I took hold of it. I remained kneeling in honor of the presence before me, the man on the throne spoke:

I, Dion of Venatici, Ruler of the Throne, King of our Tribe, declare Dominic, by order of power and virtue, the chosen one over his dominion. Angels, archangels, and principals, let it be known to all your beloved that the time to rise is now. Spread the wisdom of love and nobility. Align your people with the grace of the stars. The time has come to rank up as a whole. The time has come to join together as one living organism in a class above the rest. Prepare the human angels for the cleansing of the earth, for rejuvenation. The twelve tribes are joining together again to blast the darkness from the earth and replenish the units. Rise, Dominic, and unite the tribes.

I stood up tall with a newfound power and determination. I was granted Stella's companionship in addition to my scepter, and Stella inherited an antenna, set to the same frequency as the orb upon my scepter for way of direction telepathic communication, like walkie-talkies on the channel of clairvoyant vibrations.

I sent blessings to and through the angels and archangels working on earth on behalf of our tribe. Immediately they distributed themselves around the globe, having a revision set in motion. My messages informed me of a blockage backing up a portal, like a traffic jam stalled on the highway. This message was specifically for me because I was the cause of this buildup. My presence was needed on earth. And just as my luck would have it, I was going back to my hometown of New Orleans. I knew this had to be done sooner or later, and at this rate, the sooner the better.

Stella and I made our way through portals from Stella's connections in the cosmos. Stella's presence was a direct connection to the constellation of Canis Major and Canis Manor, which detoured its way to a link with earth, basically a shortcut when traveling through galactic dimensions. The travels would be and will be faster without this buildup in the New Orleans vortex, that of which I was accountable for.

The good news was, as soon as I'd mend this old wound, attachments would instantaneously bond in the cosmos to light up the night's sky as something of great magnitude. Like connecting the dots, treaties will be made, stars will realign, and millions of souls shall be free. The bad news was that such a change came with price, and the price was millions, even billions, of souls to be freed, generations of trapped beings haunting human souls down their own bloodlines. Humans of the earth were going to pay that price by sacrificing their lives for the evolution of mankind as a whole.

For every action, there is an equal and opposite reaction, but the truth of the matter is, lives must be taken to give new life to the whole. There is a funny paradox of bloodshed being inevitable, however unacceptable to most human minds. It's where the fear of the fear comes in. The actions and mindsets of mankind under the direction of their hierarchy has set planets and galaxies off course, imbalanced constellations, which is causing the core of the problem on Planet Earth decaying from its own cancer.

Never before had the gods seen such destruction, climbing rates of suicide, disease, and war. It became what was once an open portal for galactic friends of the cosmos and celestial bodies, a perfect circle to cycle through the universe, to a reformed pyramid. It was intended to live in GLEE, Goldie Locks Experiment of Earth, where billions of humans were created equal to live in harmony with animalia and plantae kingdoms to unite and thrive in accordance to the lowest realms of consciousness also known as hell. My mission was to stretch the gap, expanding to a new realm for soul's connection.

Every being, every building, every city, every planet and every universe has ebb and flows. Human lungs expanding and contracting, waves of the ocean flowing in and out, cities building up prosperously to crumble down, Planet Earth with species thriving and species becoming endangered or even extinct, and so on. There is a cycle for everything, every life force and source.

Humans on Planet Earth have built themselves up for a breakdown. Billions of human souls are trying to ascend to a tiny higher peak when naturally a ray of light expands out. Emotions have shifted in reverse by the mentality of greed and selfishness. The energy of light from the earth is dimming from the celestial stand-point. Programming the subconscious to limitation in the pyramid sense has humans under the control of tunnel vision. That is about to change.

Stella and I arrived in New Orleans at the scene of the crime. We could feel the tension in the air, shaking below the ground.

"What are we looking for here?" I asked Stella.

With one look, Stella connected to a different time frame. *The 1980s*, she communicated to me. I knew at that instant where we were going. The energy field around me shook rapidly, like the human nervous system on the verge of vomiting.

With the authority of my scepter, I was able to delegate my travels through the dimensions of time. I jabbed the scepter into the ground to unveil the events of 1982.

This was a big year for me. I grew up in Kenner, Louisiana, a suburb of New Orleans. I was a middle child with a brother and a sister older and a brother and sister younger than me. It felt like the first ten years of my life I had been competing for my parents' attention, for anyone to notice me. My parents worked hard to provide us with a good life. My father had worked his way up to lieutenant of the New Orleans's police department, and my mother was a professor at LSU.

This year was the biggest nightmare and the fuel of my rage. How big of an impact it created, well, I was about to find out. Stella narrowed down the time frame into specific events. I swore I would never relive this again, but thus, the reason for healing.

It was the early '80s. My oldest sister, Ranae, was sixteen at the time and just got her license but stayed home that day to babysit despite it being summer break from school.

I was in the front seat of our station wagon with my mom on our way home from court. That day I testified against my former school teacher on behalf of myself and dozens of other classmates for his inappropriate fondling and sexual acts with minors, very young minors. Not all those affected by the forceful and threatening acts came forth. I didn't have the courage for a long time either until one day I became more scared to go to school than I was to admit the shameful behavior. So a few months prior to the court day, I had told my parents about the violations and my fear of going to school after they called me out for faking sick. My father, being a police officer, didn't take it lightly. Also, my mother, being a teacher herself, was beyond disgusted, and I felt disgusting. I didn't know of any way to take those events back, reclaiming my innocence lost, but to come forth and have it stopped once and for all. My dad used his power to make sure that happened.

Driving home from court that day was the starting point for a system shutdown, which had the potential to take a much-different course. We were driving into Kenner from New Orleans, my dad following behind in his squad car.

The energy of the car was heavy, like something was pulling on me trying to weigh me down. My thoughts circulated disappointment and fear that my parents were mad at me for allowing this to happen. *What could I have done differently to stop this from ever happening to me and my friends?* I thought.

A classic Motown hit was playing on the radio that I knew all too well. I could feel a part of me reaching out to the song for liberation from these repetitious feelings I was praying would go away forever. I sang along in my head to distract myself.

Sugarpie, honeybunch / you know that I love you
I can't help myself / I love you and nobody else

My mother turned down the radio. It seemed like she wanted to tell me something but froze in shock as we both witnessed a commercial airplane dramatically descending, crashing into trees, continuing into a neighborhood in Kenner, a few blocks from our house.

A Pan Am Flight had crashed, killing 145 onboard, plus others on the ground. Stella and I exchanged information as we watched the recap. We were viewing it from a different standpoints this time, obviously. We saw how many angels were involved with the exact co-ordinance of the plane in relation to lives that were taken and who were spared. Whether I liked it or not, it was divine order.

Angels placed themselves in children's bedrooms, shielding eye-witnesses of flying debris. We replayed the scenario from many perspectives, watching the significant effect it had on me at the time and why I was feeling weighed down.

The song playing on the radio rested in my head, planting the power of words into my subconscious. The words "I can't help myself / I love you and nobody else" made a home, staying as residual energy I projected, carrying through the rest of my life, which limited me to believe that I could only love one being at a time.

It made me believe that they could only love me too and nobody else, rippling out to my experience cycle of affairs in marriage and gathering resentment, attracting more and more events to feed that resentment, validating my limiting beliefs. It limited my capacity for love. It blocked connections that could have set me on a course to help this world be in a much-better situation than it was now. I even had the potential to open up opportunities for black actors to take on more starring roles in action movies so I, too, could join in on as more than a stunt double, expanding growth in all sorts of ways.

My projection in that one moment sent out a ripple, impacting that whole area with a darkness that hovered over it like a blanket. And yes, Hurricane Katrina could have been avoided. Nevertheless, the events built up to that day in that space was inevitable.

Contrary to the guilt I had for being courageous by speaking up about my teacher abusing his power, another shift had occurred. Putting a stop to the molestation and taking that opportunity to communicate that something was wrong took a lot of courage, creating a ripple. It also sent out a ripple of connection through trust and communication, disrupting the flow of fear that could have affected more children in the future.

One big thing remained, Stella brought to my attention, and that was the twelve different nationalities on that flight were stuck because of my lack of connection I left in the moment to cycle in negative space.

I sent a message out to my highest-ranking archangels who carried the message down the line. It only took a second or so to spread the word throughout the kingdom. In the cosmic realm, time felt different. What would be a month on earth, with the rotation of the sun and moon, was all in a day's work in the celestial field. When a gamma ray burst on the other side of the galaxy or solar flares occurred, we felt it instantly while sometimes humans hardly noticed the effects it had on their psyche.

All angels on deck, the shift was about to take place. As soon as Stella and I flipped the switch, connecting the twelve tribes at the crash site, each angel paired up hand in hand with archangels would be escorting these human souls back to their inherited blood-line, connecting constellations, forming peace treaties between celes-tial bodies. The gods had waited a long time, so to speak, for this moment. Some of them took it personally as though humans had taken their families hostage, holding them earthbound by guilt, and thus the war in the cosmos.

The message came back from Archangel Gabriel, *All angels and arches in place. We are ready when you are, Captain.*

Stella turned to me, confidently tilting her head down to aim her antenna at my descendant in the car trapped in time. I set out my intention to that moment in time, aiming my scepter, aligning with Stella's antenna.

Three, two, one, go to the light! Golden lights shot out from my scepter and Stella's antenna, forcing the cycling ripple back in time like a tidal wave in the ocean, unveiling human souls weighed down under a storm cloud. Angels rushed in urgently, pulling the trapped souls away from the earth like pulling weeds out by the roots before the shadows could grab them and hold them down. Archangels were standing by with sword and shields to cast out any shadows from the underground that dare to challenge this altering moment.

Outnumbered and overpowered, the shadows sunk back down in the earth's surface, trembling. The angels took advantage of the sun's rays. With the light beaming down, the angels were able to lift off, blazing trails out of the atmosphere undetected by human eyes. I had taken back my guilt through reclaiming my courage. The under-ground, on the other hand, was sure to catch word of this. It was only a matter of time before they would take this out on the human remaining on earth. Where fear is created, it will remain until it is faced and healed with love and acceptance.

Up in the ethereal realm, a celebration was taking place as constellations were lighting up, welcoming their loved ones within their bloodlines back home.

Like shooting stars connecting dots in the sky by a golden thread, celestial bodies linked up, connecting portals to one another, constellations and families made ties for direct contacts, uniting the twelve zodiacs as a giant unit in rhythm, like they were ready for this song to be written and composed. Gods on high united and rejoiced.

On the other side of the spectrum, this rapid alignment in the cosmos rippled out a tidal wave of energy heading back toward earth. What this means for humanity is that those who continue to fight and struggle with their own, those who try to dominate over plantae and animalia kingdoms will inevitably be cast into the darkness. For those who choose peace on earth and good will to all life forces among them will be spared to stay and replenish the earth, the new world.

It is now written in the stars. It is in the hands of free will and fate (from all thoughts everywhere). Say your prayers and stay on the path of light and love. Angels hear your prayers and thoughts as they send prayers on your behalf, rippling back to you. Will you answer their call?

I dedicate my song to all my brothers and sisters taking on their lives with love and courage.

IT'S A WAY OF LIFE

A Black Belt is one who will do what it takes to stay alive—
expecting and accepting a better way of life / every day they
wake up and try to step up their game, letting go of their old
ways while hanging on to their roots, stretching for a better
view with the will, persistence, patience, drive, and hunger
for truth carrying faith, in a vision for the best and letting go
of the rest that grows stronger every second on the quest.
A Black Belt's passion fuels the fire to climb the next mountain to find
the best view. Burning our fears through the sweat and tears, we pick
ourselves back up with stronger balance between patience and flame.
A Black Belt's mind thrives on peace of mind—in balance with the
rage inside. It takes great courage to accept the greater you. It takes
great patience to seize a new day as opportunities to make peace with
their past, giving their lives right now to blaze trails, shedding skin to
better themselves for a better world rippled out for a new generation.
Never underestimate the next challenge—while respecting
its strengths and weaknesses. Stay open to make room for
improvement. Stay flexible like water to seize the moment—know
that everyone's 100 percent looks different, but in accordance to
their vibration—learning in different forms of translation.
Be merciful to your enemy's pain, remembering what there
is to gain as we all train. Stay grounded, for your roots come
so far for you to be here today, sharing your wisdom in
the way they did for you. Be yourself—knowing that your
mission intertwines with others, like a magical ocean always
in motion aligned with the moon in tune with you.
Remember that mountains and rivers can be moved. Remember,
we learn to fight on the foundation of respect and discipline—We
learn to fight for peace of mind and keep calm in order to see that
we all have a Black Belt inside. Know thy self, know thy strengths
and weakness. Know when it's not worth the fight. Know that it's
not a matter of wrong or right. Strengthen the core and you shall
find—the balance of the one who fights the battle inside for peace of
mind for mankind—acknowledge that we all have a warrior inside.

CHAPTER 11

On the Other Hand

Staring out the window of our farmhouse to rolling hills on the out-skirts of Chattanooga, Tennessee, my mind traveled to image nation. With eighty years down the drain, widowed twice, one child passed on, one loving and faithful son and two daughters who can't wait for me to pass on so they can sell the farm just to redeem the money. I have many memories to reflect on.

Born in 1938 in Murfreesboro, Tennessee, as Sarah Williams, the youngest of four children, I always felt like the black sheep of my family. My parents were strict. Well, my mother and stepdad, that is. My real father was killed overseas by the Germans in 1943. My mom remarried a farmer outside of Kansas City as soon as possible to help raise us kids.

My older brothers and sister moved out right after high school, married or went on to college, and I couldn't blame them. Being told everything I did that came naturally to me was wrong developed resentment toward my parents. By the time I was a teenager, I decided that I didn't want to live the same way my parents lived their lives. In a lot of ways, I didn't, but in some ways, I did and hadn't noticed until now.

The thing was, my mom did the best she could, providing the circumstance. Raising four children alone in the forties with little work experience and the hopes to provide her children with a good life while suddenly widowed, I can only imagine at the time would have been scary. Growing up a Christian, I did recognize some truths being taught to me that I instilled inside me to this day. One of them was divine order. I believed in honoring our roots, our family and ancestors, and on the other hand, I had a belief in individual spiritual connection with purpose. Thus, my life took me on quite a journey.

I really found myself in college. I mean, literally found myself in college at Vanderbilt University from 1956 to 1960. Since my mother wouldn't let me have any pets at home, I studied zoology for my major, and since my stepdad grew hay to feed the cows that he eventually slaughtered and sold off the meat, I became a vegetarian and minored in botany. That was where I met and fell in love with my first husband, Jonathon.

A paradox indeed, but the way I see it, a human life is trial and error, and I learned a lot on how "not" to do things. On the other hand, I also experienced in such a way that I might understand my mother and her way of life that gave this world my life. I just didn't know then what I knew now. How could I? I was determined to live my life, and my life took me to Miami.

Sarah Williams, an English bloodline, married Jonathon Muller, a German bloodline. Perhaps another paradox, but you never know how one's choices affect everything or anything when you're in it, and we were in it. For over twenty years, we were in love. Jonathon got a job in downtown Nashville as a pharmacist for two years after graduating while I finished my bachelor's degree.

Then Jonathon accepted a job as a pharmaceutical representative for a big manufacturing company in Miami. He traveled a lot, and since I was never much of a follower, I stayed home a lot of the time with a part-time job at the zoo. Through connections I had made at the zoo, I found a hobby of breeding, raising, and showing horses. That lifestyle was flexible for me to also breed, raise, and show off my own children, Theodore, Evelyn, Monica, and Patrick. I wanted to raise them in a way that was different from my background. On the other hand, I didn't know what I was doing.

Another paradox, I raised them in the same way my mother did, just from a different perspective. I wanted the best for my kids, and I also wanted them to want what's best. Anything less than the best was not okay. That rippled out to wanting to be the best with a lingering feeling of need for having the best. I'll be the first to admit that I didn't know what's wrong or right anymore.

It's like striving to thrive without the balance of being alive, here and now, the drive to do better without the gratitude of what is now, how far we've come, and what brought us here in the first place. Yeah, I skipped a step, and finally at the age of eighty years old, I could see it clearer now, even with my aging eyes, than I did at the time. Thus, this time of reflecting my missing steps.

Jonathon was a good father when he was around. He liked to talk a lot with the kids or at the kids, telling stories of his travels. He was a great communicator if he could do all the talking, which made him great at his job, and helped me to be a great listener.

Our kids ranged from seventeen to eight when we lost Jonathon and Theo to the plane crash in Louisiana. Jonathon had business in San Diego. I booked a ticket with him to interview for a potential job at the San Diego Zoo. However, circumstances with babysitters fell through over and over again until I felt there was a reason for me to stay. With the ticket already purchased, Theodore took my place, wanting to scope out potential colleges on the west coast while his dad was working, but the flight never made it there.

Aberrations of Jonathon and Theodore stood outside the window of the farmhouse in a flower patch I had just planted earlier that morning. I chose to get a head start this season, and this beautiful April morning inspired me to get it done. Oblivious to Jonathon and Theo's presence, I cleared my mind, admiring the advent sunset falling to the top of the rolling hills where a gravestone laid in memory of Charlie, my cocker spaniel I had buried just over three years ago. Charlie passed away in the late winter, a month after his best friend, my second husband, passed on at the ripe age of eighty, the same age as I am now.

It was close to two years after we lost Jonathon and Theo when I met Roger Jackson. I had intended on expanding in the health and wellness of the animals at a Miami equestrian center, attending a holistic healing convention in Orlando. Roger, a doctor in kinesiology from Nashville, happened to attend in the hopes of adding knowledge to his medical field. He was a countryman at heart with unconventional theories and outlooks. Needless to say, these black sheep hit it off instantly.

I knew that he would be a big part of my life on the last night of the convention at a social gathering. Close to half the people that had attended the holistic meeting, speeches, and workshops stuck around for a night to wind down with music, open bar, and conversation. While most of the group used it as an opportunity to expand business and gather new clients, Roger asked me to dance.

It took me by surprise when this handsome, middle-aged doctor asked me, a middle-aged woman wearing khaki-colored jodhpur pants with my favorite dusty-rose blouse, to dance as Frank Sinatra sang, "The Way You Look Tonight."

Roger and I found out things we had in common, along with differences that we could learn and grow from, like his divorce that ended in a loss of two children who chose to disown their father under the influence of their mother, which hurt him more than he led on. He took his life experiences like stepping stones so that he might better his future and future of others from his mistakes. Plus, being a doctor working on the muscles to identify imbalances in the body's chemical and emotional energy, he understood how carrying the burden of other's choices affected the human body with an unbalanced chemical reaction which led to illness.

Roger happened to have degenerative disc disease running through his family bloodline, so he also understood the importance of a well-balanced mind, body, and soul and how the combination could perform magic when faced with the impossible or incurable diseases, like the one he faced. He did a great job maintaining a healthy body and mind, slowing down the deteriorating of his spine and nerves. Eighty years was a long life of back pain, and I admired his strength and mental stability.

At forty-four years old, my life began another journey with Roger. Evelyn and Monica didn't take to the changes while Patrick, who just turned ten, adjusted to the new family with open arms, and Roger returned the opened arms back to him.

After Roger and I married, we moved to Nashville where Roger worked at the hospital downtown. Mid-'80s in Tennessee was open for new opportunities for us. I opened up a holistic shop on the outskirts, trusting in the growth of community; I had a feeling the location was promising. The shop specialized in healing ointments, rubs, patches, and plants that aided in the healing of wounds, pain, cuts, bruising, breaks, and even stress relief for humans and animals.

Business ran well for a decade or so with steady evolvement until Patrick graduated college, using his skills to boost business into the turn of the century, and that he did. Since then, we had franchised over a dozen shops throughout the east coast, from New Hampshire down to Florida.

It was right after Patrick finished college, he came home, announcing to Roger and me during dinner that he was gay. Roger held my hand as we glanced into each other's eyes, waiting for each other's reaction. Although I could feel our older, traditional way of thinking coming up, there was a glitch filtering my response, like a scratch on a record bringing the song back to original thought. Clearly there was something to look at here. I was in shock, and on the other hand, I felt the same love that I always had for him. I would love him forever just the way he was, caring and loving.

Connecting the twitter pulsing through my muscles, thanks to my nervous system, I heard one of the most profound and rare responses I had ever experienced before. "Are you happy?" Roger asked Patrick after the news was shared.

A sigh of relief, a weight of heaviness, and release of tension dissolved in that space, bringing in a new connection of a chosen family. Roger acted as Patrick's father since he was ten. The circumstances of Patrick losing his dad at a young age and Roger losing his children when they were young opened up the space for this connection. I knew at that moment that everything was just as it should be.

The next ten years seemed to fly by with business thriving and expanding. With the help of Patrick's business-management wisdom, we had fourteen shops along the coast running like a system so that I could spend more time at home with the animals.

When Roger turned seventy, he finally gave into retirement. We bought a ranch outside Chattanooga, finding a much-needed relaxation in raising, boarding, breeding, and playing with other creatures of this land. We raised herds of cattle, horses, chickens, goats, pigs, indoor and outdoor cats, and of course, Charlie.

Patrick had long since moved out living in the southern part of Nashville, but still frequently took the drive down on the weekends for visits.

On one trip up to New York, he met his beloved Dante, a real estate developer, while opening up a shop in a great location. The shop had just opened up due to the passing of the owner, who had kids wanting nothing to do with the upkeep, which worked perfectly for us.

Dante Yung was a well-sought-after construction developer for his innovative ideas infused with traditional, oriental roots. Along with the growth of New York City, he was feeling burned out by the age of thirty-five when he took a small job renovating our store. Similar to my experience, Patrick and Dante declared their part-nership without hesitation, and Dante moved from New York to Nashville with plenty of opportunity awaiting him. Together for thirteen years now with strong, good-looking heads on their shoul-ders, I looked forward to every weekend for visits.

I was feeling anxious for their visit tonight more so than any other visit. I thought it might have something to do with their announcement of adoption in the works for their first child. My nerves were adding to the excitement of the visit taking me out to dinner for my eightieth birthday celebration. Which reminded me, I wanted to make sure the animals were fed, put in safely for the night, then invite Leo, our groundskeeper/ranch manager to come to dinner with us.

Leo Wolfhart's family was Native American, derived mostly from the Dakotas and spread their bloodline down through the United States into Mexico, and even traces to the Incas back around again.

After Roger passed, I spent the last year's focusing my time on genealogy. Something sparked a light in that direction like a thought whispered in my ear or a flower opening to bloom. I followed that light, finding that I rather enjoyed it. The evidence was scattered across the dining-room table that I walked by slowly on my way outside. Hundreds of papers and links in ancestry categorized in a time line sequenced to the best of my understanding awaited the help of my hands at the table as I walked out the back door.

I opened the door, and chills ran down my spine. In the corner of my eye, I saw a ghostly figure sitting at the dining-room table. My first instinct was a scribe from the BC era. I was looking to his back-side as I began to describe to myself what I was seeing.

I heard calming words being whispered. "Everything is okay, honey. Just keep going about your business." I felt familiar warmth take my hand gently, leading me outside.

"Roger, is that you?" I thought out loud.

Immediately the spirit vanished from the table. A shock of the unknown tugged on my conscious as Iris, our beautiful tabby cat, sprang up from her coiled-up nap on top of a stack of papers on the table, looking at the empty seat that had just been occupied. Or was it still being occupied without my notice?

"Trust the process," I heard a whisper as I turned to go outside.

"Yes!" I found myself talking out loud again as those words echoed through my memory. "Roger, I knew you were here."

Ever since Roger passed, I felt a presence, as in the sense of eyes watching over me or beside me. It was a peaceful, homey feel I had when Roger and I would sit together in the same room or enjoy a conversation. Although I didn't see him with my eyes, the lack of vision stimulated other senses that recognized Roger's energy that I now felt I was blinded to when we were together. Absence makes the hearts grow fonder, and we were quite fond of each other no matter the space in between.

I felt an urge to water the flowers that surrounded the house like a mote before I walked down to the stalls, hoping to catch Leo before he settled in for the evening. *I have time*, I thought as the tangerine sun hit the top of the mountains to the west.

Leo managed this land for decades now. The prior owners hired him on in '85. We were grateful that he wanted to stay on when we took over. Leo was a licensed vet, with his whole life's experience of farms, combined with his schooling, even though he claimed he learned something new every day working outside in the elements with the animals. Roger and I really clicked with that attitude. Leo had dedicated his life to the ranch, usually working every day well past sundown. "It is a lifestyle," he would say.

As I opened up a giant storage container that I kept large quantity of bird seed in, I heard a flock of birds chirping loudly. A small meadowlark flew in between me and the house. I could have sworn it locked eyes with me, thanking me for the food I was about to distribute. It felt like a blessing of karma from the birds.

The meadowlark flew through the perimeter of the ranch like it was under jurisdiction, chirping to every tree it passed, engaging birds of their own village, and spreading word to the rest of the colonies in the trees. They joined in on the conversation as the lark flew passed them. It sounded like a poetic tone synchronizing a harmony together as though it were the moment of the bird's musical solo in a universal song set on systematic lines, angles, and pace.

At my age, the biological clock moved like the hour hand at the slowest speed while still feeling and seeing time pass by me as fast as the second's tick tock. Might I be granted the virtue of patience by carrying on after Jonathon and Roger's death? Or was patience being forced on me at this time because I lived a fast-paced life that limited me now? I didn't know, but I could tell from the once-calm, melodic tones now speeding up that I had a sense of urgency to keep up with the tick, tock, tweet, and chirp. I felt connected to these birds in ways that I couldn't understand.

"Let me help you, Sarah!" Leo came trotting up from the corrals to help with the lifting he knew wasn't as easy as it used to be for me.

"Oh, I got it," I said as a kind gesture, knowing how hard he already worked, and saving face.

"Oh, I know you do, Ms. Jackson, but it is your birthday, and you don't get to work on your birthday. It's your day to celebrate how far you've come and rest assure in knowing there is further for you to go."

He smiled with a silent, secret confidence similar to a palm reader I went to after Jonathon's death who told me that my whole world as I knew it was about to get flipped upside down. Just when I felt like my hourglass was empty, off balanced and tipped on its side, Roger came and lifted the other side, shifting my universe into a new cycle.

"Did you just put a curse on me? I don't know how much further I can go at my pace," I remarked sarcastically.

"I just put a blessing on you," he replied in a light, joking manner.

Leo hung up the bird feeders nearby as I leaned against the storage container, enjoying the view of the ranch. He softly recited a poem.

Shedding Skin

We're emerging from cells turning to dust rising from hell. We call it jail locked in a cage reproducing thoughts, let it decay. Let it fly away. Let it be, what has been.

Let it go with the wind. You can change the world within. Let the past die. May it rest in pieces. Our shedding skin turns to stones beneath us.

Deserted sage burns clarity. My hands turn cold from ebb and flow. The desert heat burns inside me. Everything's aligned, all in God's time.

Patience is a virtue. To everyone who loved me I see myself in you and love will go on. It's all in the song we can't hear but feel. It's here to heal the pain we wronged when we sold ourselves short defined by what has been.

Let it go with the wind. The world changes within. Let the past die. May it rest in pieces. The suffering ceases as our shedding skin turns to gold it will release us.

Seize the times. Reset your mind and let it unwind. Let my brainstorm shine. Shed the old skin. Let the new world begin. Let love align.

I spoke up when I came back to reality from the trance of the poem. Leo walked back from the bird feeders to me.

"Will you join us for dinner tonight at the clubhouse?"

Evelyn reserved the convention room for the night at an exclusive members-only club in Nashville, if for no other reason than to flaunt money and flush guilt on others for the cost she paid to have the ceremony arranged, denying anyone's help when offered just to throw it back in their face that she did it all by herself. She needed the credit. *Where did I go wrong with her?* I thought.

Leo piped up, "As much as I would love to celebrate with you, I feel strongly about staying here to watch over mother and colt tonight."

After Roger passed away, I felt an overwhelming desire to breed a purebred palomino with a beautiful black stallion and, lo and behold, the most-exquisite buckskin with distinct black marking on his body. She was a full, solid caramel with sleek black mane and tail as typical buckskins bore, but her attributes were from another world. The black of her mane dropped down in between her eyes, dangling a black diamond in place of a third eye. Her legs looked like he had galloped through a puddle of paint that stained all her limbs, accentuating a diamond on her left front elbow and another on her back right kneecap. Three diamonds strategically placed like birthmarks on the mind-blowing beauty. I named her Destiny. She was five years old now and just gave birth to her firstborn son three days earlier that we named Legend.

With the cold front rushing through, he made sure that the animals of all shapes, sizes, and ages stayed warm. I could tell that Leo was holding back information; he was holding back feelings.

"Well, you will be in good company," I suggested with the intention that he might bite on the line I just cast out.

"The way I see it," he said, "is that we all get to protect our energy space, even if it means letting go of family and loved ones." We were on the same page. "I have learned to keep a tight circle and select who can come into my circle. I fear that if I go to that dinner, I will be allowing outlaws to get under my skin again that took me so long to detoxify from."

He pulled up the sleeves of his grey thermal shirt to his elbows. On his left forearm, a tattoo of a majestic and rare black wolf. On it was a big flashy collar with the word in all caps—"Love."

Leo continued, "We all have the choice at every moment, every event, to choose to trust in love, respect, and generosity. Or trust in fear, anger, and selfishness. This reminds me to feed the wolf inside me with love returning the love that fills me every morning that I get to wake up to be with them." He explained while pointing out to the horizon at all the animals as far as our eyes could see. "And you, of course." Leo offered up a hug, slowly and gently, like he was embracing an old, brittle tree holding on in a winter's night. To my back, Leo saw headlights pulling up the long driveway, parking on the side of the circular round about in front of the house.

It was Patrick and Dante, who immediately saw us on the side of the house. At my age, I could hear my own thoughts better than the gravel rumbling, spitting backward from the tires pushing against them right behind me. Leo loosened his embrace, keeping his hands on my shoulders to turn me around to see our company.

"Oh, and them too, of course," he added, waving to the boys.

Leo held my arm, escorting me to Patrick and Dante, who barely had time to get out of their modest yet upscale Cadillac SUV.

As we were getting closer to the driveway at a pace set by me with Leo's support, he leaned into my ear before the boys were close enough to hear him whisper, "Keep these men in your circle. No matter whom tries to penetrate it or ridicule it, trust in love. It will guide your emotions like the lights on the dashboard. Trust in love."

My shoulders dropped as though they were hung up by tension strings and suddenly cut loose. It felt like he had just blessed me with a prayer to God, or his god, or whoever he believed in. I hardly had any moment to say anything, and it was probably for the best that I didn't. I was speechless. On the other hand, I had a lot of questions.

"Hello, my sons!" Leo bear-hugged Patrick and Dante then hoisted me into the front passenger's seat and shut the door.

I couldn't hear or read lips well enough to understand, but Leo was having some sort of talk with them. They all looked over at me in unison, nodding their heads and smiling. He gave another hug to the boys before we left. Dante jumped into the back seat, Patrick in the driver's seat, and we were off to the party.

The ride was smooth. I always enjoyed a nice Cadillac. We were on the freeway heading north. The sun had already set. Not quite dark, but the shadowy outlines of the trees merged with the asphalt on the road. Over to the west, the lingering light of the sun emerged from the shadow of the land, an orange orb like a flashlight under a blanket, fading into a consensual bliss of yellow to a reflective hint of green that continued its travel through light to dark shades of blue circling back in honor of the night.

Looking out to this view, my mind wandered to what we were doing and where we were going. I wondered if, once again, Patrick and Dante would be ridiculed and publicly lashed about their love for each other. It pained me to see such insults and put-downs. It saddened me to witness the lack of love to someone so loving. Would I be targeted or represent an easy target if I chose not to voice back in defense? I knew I don't have all answers and wasn't the perfect mom to meet all my children's expectations, but I tried my best from my understanding.

I shifted views to the gentlemen in the vehicle. I was unknow-ingly smiling in a peaceful paradise as I glanced back and forth at these beautiful men's soft eyes. Dante's eyes reminded me of the tran-scending sunset tonight. Emerging from his black pupils reflected shades of gold flowing in between golden to a dark-auburn brown encircled by a dark ring that would appear to be black. Dante's eyes shouted, "The sky has no limits!"

Patrick's eyes had the power to camouflage in a clear day's sky while opening the heavens so that the stars could sparkle through the daylight, like fairies dancing with the birds on the air floor. Complimented by golden hues, his eyes proclaimed, "The balance of fire and ice brings life."

For me, I had my fair share of vanity, but my vision of my own eyes had been taken for granted for so long I could use some help from another perspective to describe what could all be seen in mine.

The night I met Roger, he didn't hesitate to share his vision of me. While we were dancing, he stared into my eyes and said, "Your eyes are like an emerald burst open and got caught in a moment of time, like a picture standing still of a jewel in full bloom. Emerging from the shadowy pupil awakened a deep green, ascending through turquoise rays into a golden sunset."

I mean, I had some feel-good days and moments when I looked into the mirror and thought, *I look good*. But hearing it beyond my vision opened me up to a love with Roger I had yet to fully understand.

Patrick noticed me staring at him and Dante, who was sitting directly behind Patrick. He turned to me with a genuine smile, one that embraced the perfect balance of peace, joy, and faith of the unknown, possibly not knowing what I was thinking about while I stared at them like an obsessed stalker.

Just then, a green light appeared in the dashboard with a notification bell. It looked like a green leafy tree as a symbol of communication. It reminded me of something Leo said about emotions were like lights on the dashboard.

"What is that?" I asked curiously.

I had seen my fair share of light indicators, but this one was new to me.

Patrick fiddled with the buttons on the steering wheel as Dante explained, "It's automatically shifting into eco mode. When we are using the fuel in a well-balanced manner, such as speed, velocity, acceleration consistency, and things like that, it will set up like an autopilot for preservation, so to speak."

"Wow! That sounds high tech," I mentioned.

I was still processing the concept as a song began on the radio. It was Frank Sinatra's, "The Way You Look Tonight." I felt my body melt into the heated leather seats even though the outside was nearly freezing. "Aww," we all said in unison. Patrick turned it up just enough for peace to embrace the melody.

At that moment, I felt clear, like a clean slate, enjoying all my senses here with me now. Beyond Frank's lovely voice, I heard another familiar lovely voice. I could recognize that voice from anywhere. It was the warm, comforting voice of Roger that made me feel at home.

It was Roger in his poetic vibe. Through the melody of the song, he spoke his song out to me.

"On the Other Hand"

> From the hand of wisdom you take on the world, opened to humility. From the hand of self, knowing when to ask for help, unlocks the limits of humanity. From one hand you understand that on the other hand is me.
>
> It's the understanding between invited and divided that we are united. It's the understanding when it's best to grow from mistakes, to repair and repent to the knowing you have what it takes to prepare and prevent. Trust the process of a journey well spent.
>
> On one hand, a siren warning of harm, on the other hand a beacon igniting the charm. In one hand is strength compatible with weakness, like darkness making art of light from the other hand of night. On one hand is what you see, on the other hand is uniting with me.

The song on the radio ended. I must have stopped breathing. Once I realized where I was, I needed to gasp for air. My heart was pounding as though I just witnessed a phenomenon, or the calm before the storm came to an abrupt halt to boost acceleration, to build up momentum.

Patrick turned down the volume when a phone call came in. A personalized ringtone of the song "This Land is Your Land" rang throughout the vehicle.

"It's Evelyn," Patrick said. He could feel my curiousness of such a choice in ringtones, as I understood their relationship to be toxic. "I'll explain later," he said, reading my mind, as he handed the cell phone to Dante so Patrick could focus on the road.

Dante answered the phone. "Hello?" He took a deep breath, preparing for the anxiety on the other end.

"Um…hi. Is Patrick around?" Evelyn said in an irritated tone loud enough for all ears in the car, like she was on speaker phone.

Dante unbuckled himself, scooted into the middle, leaning in to share the conversation.

He politely replied back, "Yes. He is right here. We're on our way with Mom." That instant I felt a tugging on my heartstrings of another lonely soul reaching out for love and acceptance. I felt through Patrick's love that I might have lost a son to death, but on the other hand, I gained one too. Gifted by the hands of God with open arms, I learned blood and chosen love blended a new family.

Dante was my son, like Patrick, but by choice, choosing into love instead of fear—fear of the wrath of the fear within fear who was wearing the mask of the judge, jury, and executioner. We could all feel anxious as the verdict came back.

"Ugh, let me talk to Patrick," she said demandingly.

"He's driving right now. Do you want to talk to Mom?"

She snapped quickly, "No, I don't want to talk to *my* mom. If I did, I would have called her."

We all looked at each other, torn between shock and norm.

Evelyn and Monica detached themselves a long time ago, around the time I remarried. A bittersweet situation for a new home of blended, chosen family, and they chose out. It took a lot of pain to realize it was all well in letting go of family who was determined to hate and bound in anger for the higher good of a home praying for love.

She continued in the same aggressive tone, "Well, where are you guys? We have all been here waiting, and we have places to be. Some of us have bigger priorities."

Excusing the insults, Dante tried the form of accountability. "That's our fault. We were going over the adoption papers and printed them out to show everyone. It was Mom's birthday present, another grandchild. But we wanted to surprise everyone."

We could all feel her eyes rolling through the phone as she wittingly came back, "Oh, I'm sure we'll all be surprised about what sort of establishment adopts children to gay men."

Dante was so shocked he went limp, juggling the phone to keep it from dropping. He did a great job of keeping composed, responding with, "I don't know what you mean…"

Evelyn spoke over him. "Just quit driving like a grandma and get here quick. We all have lives to get back to."

Before Patrick could speak regrettable words, she hung up. The boys were furious! None of us in the vehicle were spared from being insulted by that conversation. We felt like outcasts being lured into a trap. It no longer felt exciting to be celebrating anything if that's what we were walking into. Now the check-engine light flashed on the dashboard.

"Who is she to put that on us? Oh yeah, she is Mrs. Perfect to Mr. Perfect who pops an enormous amount of pills on a daily just to get through the day, and the way I live my life is wrong?" Patrick vented as Dante put his hand on his shoulder for comfort.

"Honey, at the end of the day, we all live with ourselves and have to find our own peace of mind. Let's be grateful that we are who we are in this situation." Dante stated.

"I couldn't have said it better myself," I thought out loud. "Forgive her, forgive yourself, and while you are at it, forgive me too."

We all giggled to lighten the mood. We had just passed the sign of Murfreesboro when we hit a dense patch of fog. The shock hit us all at once, as quickly as taillights came within sight; it was too late to slam on the brakes.

Our Cadillac SUV smashed into the back of a semitruck and trailer, ejecting Dante from the back of our set triangle through the windshield, shifting positions in the triangle to the front of the hood. It took our lives instantly.

I had come full circle. I was born and buried in Murfreesboro. Date of birth was the same of death, full circle. Was there a point?

Some day when I'm awfully low / when the world is cold / I will feel a glow just thinking of you / and the way you look tonight.

There you are, Roger!

12 DISCIPLINES

I must admit, I let my power slip out blindly / Chemicals
controlling my mind slightly. Conforming, I tread lightly day by
day. I see it, a power inside saving me, having faith in me every
day. As I understand it, it restores the way. For the sake of my
sanity, for the sake of humanity I turn over my will, my way.
I searched myself for all that is real, of what I feel. I've been wrong
all along. I conformed to blend in. I did it again and again. I
formed my mind to believe I'm sinned. I'm damned as I am. I
failed that exam. I fell into the scene. I bought into the screen.
I believed these eyes were seeing reality. I thought I
believed in me. But I believed lowering my standards
would get me the votes. I believed the subliminal messages
beyond music notes. I believed in sanity. I believed history
repeated itself through me with what I believed to see.
Forgive me when I didn't believe in the purpose of you and
me. Forgive me for not believing that we can be what we see
in our mind's eye. Forgive me for believing what the mirror
reflects / God, clear my vision. Remove all the defects.
Remove my shortcomings. I use the space for up and comings—
make amends with my friends. Bless the less fortunate. Confessing
as I'm progressing—I admit I'm a working progress.
Relieve me of confusion. Relieve me of illusions, I
pray—close my eyes and meditate for wisdom and
strength to do what I can do today, to accept human
mistakes and bring our loved ones out of the cave.

CHAPTER 12

Bob

By far, the most illuminating sight so bright of rolling clouds in the sky with fairies farting out confetti, molding pearls twirling in a bucket of liquid paint above my head.

Trust the process, Sarah heard Roger's voice.

I do, Sarah said immediately back, having faith in the familiar tone. The pearly twirling in the sky fell upon her as she rose to see a gate between earth and ethereal realm.

Do you wish to go on a journey with me? Sarah heard another voice say.

Who are you? Sarah couldn't see a gatekeeper, but contrast of white over white, like a spotlight glaring in a mirror, beyond her glow through a dry, cloudy gust from the lingering mist, the deep-blue abyss.

Before the bridge is lowered, before we open the gate, come through please. Write me a poem, a story of your angle. Speak to the guide for me to describe the gathering of the tenth tribe.

Like a surreal dream, Sarah just went with it. *Who is the guide?* she asked.

Your guide is your personal translator, the voice responded.

Who are you? Sarah repeated.

The voice appeared to me as the answer echoed, *In honor of the kingdom, I have been your guide, and now I am the scribe.*

The scribe in my house, Sarah contemplated as the scribe stood on the other side of the foggy gate. The scribe continuously shifted in and out of human and animal forms, as if presenting its unisex wisdom of all generations—male and female, elder and baby, humans and dolphins, dogs and cats changing into bears and bunnies, all different shapes, all wearing indigo blue.

Before I lower the bridge, said the scribe, *before you come through, please read me your poem, the story through the eyes of the spirit who guides the black sheep to the light to see the bright side. Sarah, will you tell your story in your words? Share from your heart, child, the song of where you've been, where you are now, and where you are going to spread your love and learned new ways of love.*

"Sarah's Song"

"Where do I start?" Sarah says. "No, really, where do I begin? I've watched so many lives. I've lived so many lives. I've been a tree waiting patiently to see the love and smiles. I've lived so long and have seen what happens in the woods.

"Should have, could have, would have turned back time, trees have seen brutal wars for centuries to help in the realm of PTSD. I've been a girl in a snow globe world lost in a place I call my own. I've been feared. I've felt alone, and I've been afraid of the unknown. I was bruised and beaten and in my minds. As a human I can't conceive that it's all happening inside of me.

"Well, I know where I've been. I have been everywhere up until here, through the eyes of my parents and through the eyes of theirs. So many memories that our eyes have to see and so many others our eyes want to unsee. I danced and I loved, I laughed, and I hugged the rain clouds above me."

"I've searched and I found, and what I know now is there is more than enough love to go around. But, as Sarah, well, who am I? I've felt so many things. I've lived so many lives. Who am I in the midst of all of this, you ask? That song I wrote was in the past. I am here right now," Sarah says. "In ways I've always imagined in my head next to my snow globe above my bed."

Thank you, Sarah, the scribe expressed graciously.

How will I know where I'm going? Sarah asked the scribe.

And to her request, he replied, *Sometimes we don't know until we go, and others create the place by writing the show. Like a caterpillar knowing to retreat in the cocoon, you will know soon. Do you, Sarah, wish to share this journey with me? Do you want to go for a ride?*

I do, Sarah replied.

The gate dropped like a drawbridge, opening up a new world. Sarah bobbed her head, smiling as she went along with the scribe's rhyming.

Orbiting outside the Milky Way, the fog faded away like a dream upon the opening of my eyes, the eyes of Sarah. In a circular crystal orb, much like a snow globe encompassed by a lavender hue, Sarah sat at the dining-room table next to Roger inside their farmhouse nestled within the orb, flying through space. Beyond the windows were satellites, astronaut capsules, and shooting stars that appeared to be other living planets, other celestial beings relocating in the sky.

Roger was wearing overalls he had worn while working on the farm with his white doctor's jacket over the suspended straps. His head resembled Charlie's as a King Charles spaniel.

Roger, um, Charlie, what is this place? Sarah asked, confused on how to address her husband-infused dog.

Beautiful, angelic voices accompanied classical music played in the house, echoing out from Roger's hearing aid inside Charlie's ear.

The scribe began to write, and as he did, a new language of visions, graphs (of bloodlines/DNA running through veins), words, and letters scrambled to trigger specific nodes in our brain waves and expanded a world to our understanding. The scribe wrote, and as the writing went down on paper, she and Roger/Charlie watched the story unfolding outside the windows as though we were surrounded by television screens.

Our dog Charlie's great-grandfather, Woodrow, lived in England where his human companions bred him with other royal bloodlines from the Canis Minor constellation. He fathered dozens of children with multiple women, all of whom were scattered around Planet Earth, never to be seen by Woodrow again, until the afterlife.

The windows of the farmhouse became telescopes peering down on a multitude of spots on the planet where his bloodline had spread, multiplied, and transformed moving into other bloodlines.

The scribe proceeded to explain. *Through pure love and acceptance, adopted families were formed, expanding and connecting our origin of constellations, aligning celestial bodies in the cosmos.*

The top of the dining-room table that sat in the middle of the scribe, she and Roger/Charlie flashed on to a visual screen. It was a map of the universe. Constellation Canis Minor expanded out to Canis Major like limbs of a tree reaching for the sun. Constellation Canis Major embraced certain planets within Canis Minor, connecting rays, forming tunnels of light used as portals of travel and direct communication.

Along the journeys of Woodrow's offspring, bonds were made with peace treaties and vows between species.

Other links expanded out on the map to every sign in the zodiac. Naturally, Sarah identified signs that she could relate to. Pisces was her human zodiac constellation, a hometown, so to speak, that her prior consciousness passed through on her way to Earth. Gemini was where her two cats journeyed through, Jynx and Cleo. They had similar paths through the cosmos, passing in and out of Gemini to Earth and circling back around to the constellation of Lynx, their origin.

Sarah was in awe, seeing that everyone she ever knew had their own graph like a life map synchronized as though we were all meant to be a part of each other's lives, crossing paths in a quantum sequence that human brains haven't opened up to conceive. The level of consciousness was far beyond what Homo sapiens could fathom at this space in time.

Sarah couldn't help but to continue looking for Libra which, by scientific calculations, was part of Roger and Charlie's journey.

Where is Libra? Sarah asked.

We are in it, the scribe explained. *Charlie's grandmother crossbred with a Spanish cocker spaniel where one of their children traveled overseas, alongside his human companions, spreading his seeds throughout the country.*

The map on the dining-room table flickered into another scene, like changing a channel. It was a map of Planet Earth laid out on a flat screen. The bloodline's origin spread out across the whole world with all lines leading back to Woodrow.

How old is this map? Sarah questioned, due to her sense in genealogy.

Woodrow took over as king of the House of Spaniels after his father passed on in the plague. This kingdom was also known as the black sheep.

Sarah watched everything said play on screen.

Every bloodline is written and placed in the sacred realm of Akashic records. Every generation in a family is granted a scribe as a translator and medium to help connect the bloodlines according to connections on earth and some connections go far beyond blood, as you can see.

Sarah did see. It was far beyond what she imagined as a human. On the other hand, her love for her animal companions brought her here now. Sarah began to put all the information together.

So what are we doing in Libra? How does Libra connect to all of this if we are in it? Sarah wondered.

The scribe wrote, and as the writing went down on the paper, the table turned back to the map of the universe showing galaxies intertwining into the next one through one portal or more, connecting stars and constellations through the cosmos.

We are going to a safe house, in a galaxy forming around Canis Major and Canis Minor called Canis Manna. This planet is called POA. It is there that you can help write the story. Through my connections, I will translate all information to all celestial beings. It is through your connections bonded with Roger and Charlie in Libra that I may translate to you. As a human, I came from Spanish descendants traced back in accordance of the Libra constellation and male writer, derived by translation into Libro, meaning, "book." With your connections with animalia and experience of genealogy, I appreciate the help from you, Sarah, to write this book for the records. Your mission, Sarah, should you choose to accept it, is to gather information through your bloodline's adopted family to unite and reunite the animalia kingdoms, the scribe explained

Sarah's love overpowered any thought that would question the mission's intention. *I do accept*, Sarah said graciously.

Roger lifted Sarah's hand up to Charlie's face. Charlie licked it clean and, to Sarah's surprise, turned not just her hand but whole lower body into a horse, resembling a female centaur. She accepted and adapted quickly to her transformation.

She glanced down to the screen of the dining-room table to see the reflection of herself. Sarah's chest was covered by her favorite dusty-rose blouse while a body of a horse still managed to squeeze into the pleated skirt she was wearing as a human. Charlie leaned down, reflecting his tender gaze, smiling at her as she processed herself.

I still managed to keep my head on straight, Sarah joked as the table turned back into the handcrafted wooden table that Leo had made for them as an anniversary gift. *How do I communicate to you? I mean, how do I do everything that needs to be done?* Sarah asked the scribe.

It's all in divine order. We will cross that bridge when we get there.

Fair enough, Sarah thought. *So what are we doing now? What do I call you?*

The scribe smiled at Sarah as they penetrated the atmosphere of POA. "Here we will write the *Book of Black* Sheep. You can call me Bob."

THE SCRIBE

In regards to your life and what it's worth, you were forgiven
the moment of birth—a life created to make this earth a piece
of you, to make peace with you, to have and to hold.
This story is about you. You asked for it and you got proof in
moments of truth you heard God inside you speaking through
the air, seeing through your unaware ego that exits God out.
Without a doubt, you are the reason this story is written in
the stars that remind us our Angles honor the scars of those
who have been bitten by the beast of fear. It's all here. Dust
your lenses to see clear, to forgive what's on your mind. Seek
it out and ye shall find a blemish as a guiding light, and let
yourself the time to heal the OCD that overcomes destiny by
the power of love from your ancestry, forever infinitely.
Forgive yourself of asking for help by Angels awaiting the
call. Forgive mistakes and the hands of fate that catch you
when you fall. It's inside us all and all around, from ground
to sky, love can be found if that's what you look for.
As a guide and your scribe, I see every door, in every language
told. I see every thought, every word to the stories you
withhold. I see the way you compete against humanity,
when the word, "compete," roots deep that mean "striving
together in harmony." It is through you, God sees.
As a guide and a scribe, I listen and speak silently on the papers
prepared for your life eternally, forever and always writing
stories of glories in history to the mystery of our being. Seeing
you, and still seeing through gives life a great meaning.
I thank you for taking on your life the best way you knew. I thank the
mother's nature to nurture and fathers for planting the seed that grew
champions, being terrestrials. I thank God for giving celestial beings
time to help heal the PTSD that humans and animals feel in part of
the story described about the connection of the unwritten tribes.
And so I write for you, and everyone you knew, potential that
Sarah desensitized for the sake of poetry the scribe describes.

CHAPTER 13

CBT

It was written in the records that a strong alliance between Canis Major and Canis Minor was formed centuries ago in the cosmos and Canada when Sir Chewy, a black Newfoundland dog with a white diamond patch on his chest, adopted a Jack Russell terrier named De-De into his family with Homo sapiens.

In the Alberta providence, Sir Chewy worked on a farm as a protector of the other species that were working together for the cause of the farm's production and livelihood. Coming from a different background of culture with added-on history of abuse, caged-up neglect, and abandonment issues, or tissues, De-De was grateful to have a new home. On the other hand, she feared that at any time, she might be hit, abandoned, or caged up again just for living the only life she knew, just for being her.

That wasn't the case for this new adopted and adapted family. Though it took years of practice, patience, and CBT, *c*ognitive *b*rain *t*herapy, conditioning by trials, catching before terminal, concentrating beyond translation, calculating best theory, or choosing to be together, they bonded a close family.

Chewy, being the biggest of the canines, communicated well with the horses, cattle, and of course, took really great honor in the duty of being the protector of the sheep in between any time he could swim in ponds or lakes nearby. That was one of Sir Chewy's favorite things to do.

Among Chewy and De-De's farm family were horses, chickens, cattle, sheep, goats, fish in the pond, and the Homo sapiens. Harold and Hannah were the owners of the farm inherited by Harold's parents after they passed on. Harold grew up in a split family where his dad was left with three children to raise when his wife died while giving birth to the third baby.

Overwhelmed with the mourning of his wife and the responsibilities that came with kids put him in a dark place. He felt he had no control over his life, confused on what to do with his circumstances. So he did what a lot of people would do, and that was find another mate to help and hopefully want what he had to give.

Harold's father remarried, having another child to add to the family, which was Harold.

The sitting arrangement at the dining-room table was no longer accommodating to Sarah's lower body to take a seat. She stood by in the mobile orb-flying farmhouse as the scribe, Bob, collected papers individually that were now back on the table. It was Sarah's genealogy papers she had left with her house cat, Iris, before she left to the birthday party that she never made it to.

As Bob was collecting these papers one at a time, they flew off the table into his infinite tablet of wisdom he placed in front of him, like some kind of Mary Poppins book that could hold anything and everything you put in it.

The scribe continued to change shape and form from human to animals as he, sometimes she, described the story playing out on the window screens. The whole time throughout the story, Sarah had a question building up in thought. Sarah also felt she was embodying the feelings, emotions, and thoughts of all the characters as though she had been there. *How does all of this connect to me?* Sarah questioned.

Bob took a pause in the story to address Sarah's concern. *I'm glad you asked*, he stated. Roger/Charlie got up from their seat, stretched, and walked over next to Sarah, placing his hand on Sarah's lower back where it joined together with her animal spirit, rubbing back and forth like a human would pet an animal.

Energy ignited Sarah's being as if centuries of molecules built up in Charlie and Roger had been released into her instincts. Every thought that they had consumed, that their ancestors passed on to them had imprinted into Sarah's consciousness.

CBT: communicating by telepathy, communicating by thought.

Sarah felt a rush of energy flowing through her vortex like she had been born again from dying millions, even billions, of times before while flowing back her accumulation of thoughts and feelings on to Roger/Charlie. Hormones built up from Roger/Charles blood-line surfaced as pheromones radiated into Sarah's spine, going up her back like a portal to her brain, triggering Sarah's hormones, making its way throughout her body, illuminating out pheromones through her hooves into the hardwood floors, spreading into everything in sight, brightening up everything in her traveling snow globe.

Suddenly everyone and everything in the farmhouse was on the same page as the scribe.

This is your other hand, Sarah, Bob explained. *While some relationships are broken by vows of "until death do us part," Roger and You vowed forever, like some other families do. These promises and vows are written in record as declarations for your next life. You're a shooting star right now, relocating to a place chosen for you, by you, for your next evolutionary experience. We're heading to your place of adaption, POA.*

Just those words triggered memories within her subconscious. Another hormonal release burst open in Sarah's mind like a treasure chest with a rusty lock broke out. A rush and flush of serotonin dispersed throughout Sarah's energy field, more than enough to send any human on earth into a panic attack. The energy filtered down her body, and Sarah began to feel a new sensation. Her tail lifted up as a whole pile of manure was released on to the hardwood floor.

More shocked than embarrassed, Sarah had another question a rise. *How did I do that? I thought I was just a soul. How am I still alive in this body?* Charlie influenced Roger's body to bend over and take a few whiffs of manure exposed on the floor of their dining room. The aroma flew through the house as the scribe directed the air to flow his way.

As Bob inhaled pheromones, some toxic and some harmonious, he immediately went back to writing as though he were filling in gaps of a story he had been writing for ages and apparently the manure had something to say. With everyone in the room on the same page, Sarah already knew the answer.

Well, I'm glad I can help with the process, she joked.

She knew that through her process, she had a rejuvenating system within her to help the growth of everyone involved. Now that that information had been processed, she wanted to learn more. She could understand familiar emotions and thoughts she had experienced before, finally ready to process it now, and she wanted to dig deeper to get under what she didn't know yet. Or so she thought she didn't know.

Bob jumped into her thought process, but like everything out there (referring to the window-watching), the answers were in here. He referred to all the papers scattered on the table. Another trigger went off in Sarah.

The papers turned into puzzle pieces. Someone or ones had been working on this puzzle. Some parts were pieced together in big chunks, revealing portions of the big picture; some had a few to several pieces bunched up, and others were scattered by the single pieces. All pieces were equal and important part of the picture, and all carried their own story.

The scribe rapidly changed identities of all individuals whose life stories were on the table, changing so fast Sarah could barely keep up, but everyone struck a familiar sense that resonated within her. He stopped and embodied the life of Harold as he telekinetically tossed a connected group of puzzle pieces at the window. That part of the puzzle played out through the windows, and as it did, Sarah knew from the depths of her being that she was watching herself through the eyes of herself. She could feel every thought, feeling, and emotion of all the characters in the scene, and CBT took affect again, coming back together. To solidify her validation, she watched the window screens.

Harold grew up with connections and disconnections among his family. He felt a great sense of love and gratitude from his parents,

Christine and Robert, who met when Christine—going through an alcohol-induced, abusive marriage finding its way to divorce—moved to Alberta for a new life. Looking for a job, she came upon a Ma and Pa shop selling farming supplies, which incidentally was in need of a Ma to help run it.

It clicked, and the rest was history, until now it became the future.

Harold was raised feeling like a favorite of the two parents in a sense of hope for a renewed life from his father and appreciation from his mother as a direct connection into the already-established family. On the other hand, his half-sisters and brother resented all the attention he got from his parents, and Harold turned into a product of the repercussions.

George was the oldest son. Amelia and Mary were the fraternal twin sisters in the middle, and Harold the youngest. Originally born a citizen of the United States from South Dakota, George enlisted in the US Army to fight in the Civil War, dying in a battle outside of Jamestown, Virginia. He brought with him PTSD from his mother's death in the complication of Mary's birth. Those effects didn't stop there nor were they left with his lifeless body in Virginia. George's feelings held him earthbound in the afterlife to tie up loose ends. Like the gravity force that humans felt weighed down by, George was held down by guilt force of descended thoughts, which gravitated back to his family bloodline.

Harold was ten years old when that happened and had mixed feelings about it. While his father was deeply distraught with another loss in the family, Amelia and Mary took the loss as a new challenge among their ongoing strive for attention and affection of their parents, acting out in any way they could imagine to get any sort of reaction from either one. That resulted in a lot of punishment and discipline for the sisters, adding confusion with them of how to get it right and a competition between them of who could make a better life and who had better things than the other one. The loss of mother and brother tore the twins apart.

Sarah could feel her severed ties between her and her sister, rippling out to the same scenario of her two daughters and the OCD effect—offense caused by defense, overly corrective discipline, overriding control of destiny, or straight-up obsessive compulsive disorder. However, which way Sarah decided to write it in her consciousness, she could feel it in her core. She continued watching the window screens.

Harold, on the other hand, observed and felt the separation anxiety dividing his family. Under the influence of his instincts, he decided to have a new outlook while trying to honor his roots. His sisters took mostly to their Siamese twin cats, which ironically made their way to the farm as a form of peace offering to the girls on their fifth birthday.

Although Amelia and Mary never knew their biological mother, and Christine had been the only mother they knew, they were told of their mother by our father and George, who had vague memories of her. Either way they looked, they were still in the middle of it and did everything their egos told them to do in order to cope. So to help bring ease to the situation, Christine got them cats, Jynx and Cleo.

Harold played outside a lot on the farm, making friends with everyone to fill the emptiness that came with the feelings of being cast out by his big brother and sisters. That inspired him to grow up to become a veterinarian, which came in handy when he inherited the farm.

Harold and Hannah were newlyweds when they took on the ranch. His mother, Christine died in her fifties of pneumonia. Three years later, Robert died of a hemorrhage in the brain after a depressed, drunken mishap with one of the horses. The residual energy of sadness remained on the farm, affecting all lives within it somehow or another.

At the time, Hannah was raised to be a trophy wife and mother. More than anything, she looked forward to being a mother. Harold, on the other hand, had reservations about being a father. His experience brought about strong feelings of how "to be" and "not to be" a dad. He didn't know the right way to raise children, or if there was a right way; and if there was, he didn't feel capable of blending the two worlds. Did he have enough room in his heart to love a child?

That he figured out as he went on. With his love for Hannah, he did his best to accommodate her wish to be a mother. And so it was. They went on to have four children—a girl, Adeline, then twin boys, Vernon and Donald, and youngest daughter, Lillian—which went to show that love outpowered fear every time.

They had their hands full with running the farm, Ma and Pa shop, and four kids. Little did they know at the time, a whole other family was joining the mix right under their noses.

CBT

(Confused by Thoughts, Clocks Breaking Time)

We're conditioned by trials, Controlling Balls of Truth—
Correcting Behavior and Thoughts, helping Connection Between
Two. Choosing to Be Together, forever Concentrating Beyond
Translation. The expectation Climbs Both Trees, and Comes
Back Through, Conscious Because Time Comes Back Too.
Collaboration is Being Taught, while Counting
Backward Takes Time Back Cause this moment
is all we got to Collect Better Thoughts.
Communication By Telepathy Can be taken as empathy
Competing Between the one—One love Can Bring
Together, it Connects Broken Ties, Combining Brother's
Trust, Connecting Back Tribes. One love Can Be Touching,
Crushing Blows Thrusting chimes back to the future.
What does CBT have to do with me? Mastering
the mind for what it is—Choosing to Be True—
Competing by Terror, Competing Both Together.
Calculating Brain Thoughts makes nothing seem new—
Chain Breaking Traditions are not an issue, Changing
Boundaries Takes Courage Beyond Traditional views.
Cleaning the Blood Tank, Commence the Brainwash
Tactics ushering cells back through to clean out the attic.
Celebrating the Bath of Truth tied back to childhood
with a belief that these Characters Brought Together
can be together forever, is the story told by you.

CHAPTER 14

PTSD

It had been ten years since Harold and Hannah moved to the ranch when The Duke arrived. Before De-De came to the family through the blessing of Sir Chewy, Duke was in the picture. It just so happened that Duke's presence in the family prepared them to help De-De with her future memories of PTSD. Divine order, perhaps?

Sir Chewy, the ranch's Newfoundland dog, and The Duke shared the same grandfather, Koa. Koa was adopted into a Sioux Indian tribe in South Dakota when he was found wandering through the reservation after his previous human family was gunned down in their own home during the Civil War.

Koa had been courting Ruby, a great Pyrenees on a nearby farm. On the side, he also made visits with Ursula, a border collie from the closest ranch in proximity of his home north of Kansas City. Koa was coming back home from a visit with Ursula to find his home burned to ashes and residual smoke. He could still smell the burning flesh of his humans and blood boiling in the simmering coals.

Heartbroken and helpless, he made his way back over to Ursula's ranch, but the owners banished him from the property immediately when they found out about the romance between the two.

Feeling abandoned and unwanted, Koa went to Ruby's ranch. When he smelled from her pheromones that she was pregnant, it gave him hope for a family. He lived out in the barn for a month or so when the humans found out about the pregnancy by way of surprise birth. Due to the growing family, and money being tight at the ranch, Koa was released again to fend for himself. He headed north.

For months, Koa scavenged his way onto the reservation in South Dakota, where after a good sniffing and interrogation from O'nock, the chief's wolfhound, he was welcomed into the tribe. He was given to the chief's sixteen-year-old son, Maka, in honor of the gifts from the earth.

Koa gave Maka an enthusiasm about life beyond his duties of being the son of the chief. Koa was still young in spirit, as was Maka, and both found themselves with secret romances within the tribe.

Maka and his human girlfriend, Ninah, had grown up side by side on the reservation. Their friendship developed into a romance the year Koa came onboard. They had a young love that their parents weren't fond of that resulted into a pregnancy they couldn't keep a secret for very long. They had planned to tell their parents at the next full moon ceremony. While on the other hand, Koa had sparked another Canis Major romance with Ninah's dog, Ama, a Leonberger who was traded by a Canadian family for buffalo furs, also resulting in a pregnancy.

During the dancing, drumming, and peace-pipe passing at the full moon ceremony, the announcement was made about Ninah being with child. Commotion rose up with the unexpected news, but the parents of Ninah and the chief decided to take the time to accept the joining of families and planned for expansion.

The excitement and delegation happening at the ceremony distracted the tribe, prolonging the announcement of Koa and Ama's new litter until the moment of birth to their five baby puppies.

After a couple months of raising the pups, the tribe decided to trade Koa and Ama's babies out for winter supplies. Otto, the biggest of the litter, went to Robert, Harold's dad, which eventually produced Sir Chewy for Harold. All babies were dispersed out, but one. The tribe had spoken, announcing that Kongo, the smaller Newf of the bunch, stayed in the tribe.

The next year, 1863, was a year in much need of healing for the tribe. Maka and Ninah gave birth to a beautiful baby girl named Paytah, meaning fire, inspired by the bonfire of the full moon ceremony when they announced their pregnancy. That summer Koa passed away in a field outside the reservation when he frightened a herd of buffalo on a walk one day, suffering a fatal blow to the head by the wild stampede caused by the scare. The whole tribe mourned for Koa's death.

Kongo, still being a young pup of one year old, and his mother, Ama, who had just turned five, decided to carry on Koa's legacy, having a litter of pups together in the fall of 1863. Before winter hit, that litter of pups was traded out; again one pup remained with the tribe, Duke. Also known as Hotah to the tribe that meant "grey or brown," and in Duke's case, it meant grey. Duke got his color from his mother that had been very rare within the litters of mostly black, a few with little grey patches, but none fully grey like Duke, the Hotah.

Ama and Kongo made it through that winter, warming Hotah in the middle of the nightly snuggle bundles. O'nock, the chief's wolfhound, was a sucker for sticking to his roots, which meant he joined in on the dog pack's snuggle at night when he wandered from his tent.

The next spring, during the time of the spring solstice, the tribe had gathered around the fire for a full moon ceremony. Maka and Ninah shared the joy of their one-year-old, Paytah, while Kongo and Ama watched nearby as Hotah got out his six-month-old testosterone dance and tail-chasing celebration in the wheat field on the side of the village close to the party.

The bonfire was big enough to light up the surroundings for everyone to have room to play and dance, keeping most everyone in sight. In the midst of the peace-pipe passing, Duke caught a whiff of outsiders. Pheromones blew in the wind like a stench of massacre and rage. Duke tucked his tail between his legs and ran back to camp.

O'nock began to bark toward the south of the reservation. Kongo and Ama joined in on the warning and defense. As a sure sign of intruders, the tribe instantly stood up on guard to check out what the commotion was all about. Before the tribe could prepare to defend their ground and families, a clan of infantry soldiers came in hot. Parents ran around frantically to gather children and hide in tents and weaved huts.

O'nock ran toward the gunfire. He managed to scalp the arm of one of the soldiers before he was struck by a bayonet straight through his heart. His lifeless body laid in the field, getting trampled by incoming soldiers on foot and horse.

Kongo, Ama, and Hotah could clearly sense the smell of soldiers from the south and east. With young Hotah's little experience of survival, they told him to go hide at the north of camp. There was a mountain range close by with rocky cliffs, and they would meet him there. It took a moment of convincing, in the middle of guns, screams, fires, and their tribe falling dead to the ground all around them, before Hotah ran away from camp, never to return again.

Kongo and Ama nuzzled Hotah a loving nudge, urging him on his way. He was more than a hundred yards away when he heard a whining howl of pain from his mother, which made Hotah run even faster.

He made it to the mountainside. It was dark around him with a glimmer of light reflecting off the rocks from the full moon. A distant light of the village from the massive fires burned down the homes of his family, illuminating in the distance.

Paytah survived the raid in the arms of her deceased mother near the bonfire. By the mercy of Frank Williams, a soldier that lost a baby girl in his own story of a forbidden love, took her in after giving word to the other soldiers that he would sell her off as a slave.

After witnessing the deaths of his human family and mother/ wife, Ama, Kongo escaped to the south west as soldiers surrounded and torched the village. Confused, scared, and disoriented by the attack, Kongo couldn't make out a direct scent of Hotah. Smoke, gunpowder, pheromones, and blood polluted the air around him. Kongo kept running, scavenging his way into the Rocky Mountains of Colorado.

Hotah waited most of the night for any signs of his parents. Any noticeable gust of wind or crackle in the trees kept him awake. Stressed and exhausted, he hiked up to a small plateau near a cove of the mountain and curled up into a ball. Not long after Hotah dosed off, he was woken up by a mother bear in defense mode. Even at a young six months, Newfoundlands could grow well over one hundred pounds; and to a new mother bear, that could seem like a threat. Hotah scuffled to his feet at the roar of the bear and instinctively ran for his life.

Through the spring into the summer, Hotah made his way northwest into the Canadian territory of Alberta. For months of travel, Hotah would pick up the slightest scent of family blood flowing through the air. Hotah's best guess was to follow the direction of the smell. One day Hotah hesitantly came upon a farm with aromas of food surrounding it.

Sir Chewy stood guard on the porch for the best view of the entire farm. Accustomed already to the fragrance of the farm, Sir Chewy noticed an unknown yet familiar scent coming in closer. He searched the perimeter visually and spotted something grey in the field behind their red barn. He verbally notified Harold of the intrusion and ran out to encounter Hotah.

Sir Chewy came to an opening in the tall grass where Hotah was crouching on all fours. Hungry and scared, he begged for mercy, stating that he meant no harm and fell into submission. Sir Chewy did a thorough inspection of every scent he could make out of Hotah's experience. Within those scents, he could smell the scent of family blood.

You descend from Koa, Sir Chewy said to Hotah. Hotah stood up slowly and agreed. Realizing the generation separation, they nuzzled heads and walked together to the farm.

Harold was waiting on the porch, watching Sir Chewy walking through the grass line with his new friend, his long-lost nephew, with the mannerism of declared adoption. Sir Chewy already decided that they were keeping him.

Hannah and the young children came out to see what the barking was all about. Harold went into veterinarian mode and began to check Hotah out for wounds, visual disease, or infections.

"Who is this?" Hannah asked in front of the kid's curious excitement.

"I don't know, but what are the odds, two Newfs?" Harold said as he stood up, being satisfied with his inspection.

Sir Chewy sat next to Hotah as though saying, "I'm not coming back into the house without him."

The two Newfoundlands sat side by side on the grass, staring back at the family.

"Can we keep him?" The kids shouted with enthusiasm.

Harold noticed a worn-down necklace around Hotah's collar line. Next to it an old, dried smudge of blood on his shoulder. The necklace resembled an Indian filigree neck ring. Hotah appeared to have outgrown it, choking up on his jugular and carotid artery.

"Well," Harold said to the kids. "If the owner comes looking for him, we will do the right thing and give him back, but in the meantime..." He knelt down in front of the dogs. "In this family, we like to address each other formally, so from now on, you will be known as The Duke."

The kids celebrated with joy, running down the porch steps to greet The Duke into the family.

That night, The Duke insisted on sleeping on the cool ground below the stairs of the porch. Sir Chewy, who had his own blanket folded up on the floor in the living room, kept him company at the top of the porch steps in the archway of the white railings. As Duke drifted off to sleep, Chewy watched him weep, triggering muscle memory of running in terror. Chewy tapped into the vibration of abandonment and pain of loss coming from Duke. In the three years of Sir Chewy's life, along with his human Harold's work as a vet, he had experienced loss as well. Not in such a traumatic way as The Duke but enough to sense the hurt inside.

The next morning, Harold made a clean cut to remove the Indian filigree collar around Duke's neck. As a sign of respect, he wrapped it around the white railing of the porch on the left side of the archway. Then Sir Chewy followed Harold to the barn to feed the other animals. Duke took it upon himself to follow a short distance behind with his head hanging as close to the ground as it could get for a giant dog.

When Harold opened the barn door, Duke lifted his head; and in the corner of his eye, he saw a male and female duck dive down from the sky, landing in the pond that was used for the farm's watering hole. As far as Duke knew, one of his duties was to chase the ducks out of the bushes or water so that his tribe could eat dinner. Instinctively he darted over to the pond, scaring the ducks back up to the sky. Sir Chewy followed behind him, growling.

He snapped at Duke on the shore of the pond and scolded him for disrespecting the farm family. He didn't understand that way of living and never had a pond to swim in, for that matter.

Sir Chewy disregarded his normal chores of following Harold around as he did his animalia doctor rounds and stall checks. He knew that Duke was in need of rehab from his PTSD—paranoid traumatized soul demons, potential to spread disease, power to sense dimensions, path through severed doors, Pharaoh tracking source of depression, and the classic post-traumatic stress disorder. The Newfs took a swim in the pond to wash off the dried blood and built-up dust and debris in Duke's double coat. That opened up a new sense of pleasure within him that raised his vibration with hope.

Sir Chewy taught him about how the farm works, along with the rules and boundaries set between the species. Every species and kingdoms had their own set of rules, and at this farm, there was a mutual respect of everyone's place and an alliance to protect each other like family did. That's how this family worked anyway. Sir Chewy introduced Duke to the ducks of the pond, Ralph and Frannie, the chickens that lived there in harmony with the goats, sheep, horses, and cattle.

This was a whole new world for Duke. Although he missed his family dearly, he felt lucky that there was a loving, welcoming family to be with until he met back up with his tribe. He hadn't given up hope that he would see his mom and dad again.

For the next couple of nights, Duke remained at the bottom of the porch stairs. Sir Chewy was patient and understood that Duke had never been in a house such as this before, let alone have a staircase to climb. One evening Harold and Hannah came out to the front porch to check on the dogs prior to bed.

"He still won't come up the stairs?" Hannah asked Harold, assuming he knew all the answers about animals.

"Not yet," Harold replied, sparking an idea in him. Harold ran into the house and back out quickly with a piece of jerky. He split the piece in half for an equal share for Chewy and started to call Duke.

Duke sat up and looked up toward the porch. He smelled the jerky that had a similar smell to the jerky his tribe shared with him.

"Come on, Duke!" Both Hannah and Harold expressed excitedly.

Duke tilted his head to the new words spoken, watching Chewy stand up next to them, supporting the invitation. Chewy translated the new language for Duke as he connected the feeling of intention to it.

Duke also saw the apparitions of his mother, Ama, and Ninah, his human mother who made him his collar wrapped around the railing. Transparent, they levitated on the porch next to his new family. Ninah smiled, waving her hand over, as if to say, "It's okay to go inside. We're here with you."

Sir Chewy ran down the stairs to take the steps with him. Slowly and hesitantly Duke climbed those four steps, took the jerky gratefully, and followed the family into the warm house.

The next three years, Sir Chewy and Duke worked side by side on the farm, and from time to time, they would take a dip in the pond. Duke respected the ducks on the premises. They also took steps of releasing the PTSD by practicing the skills determined, practicing to see differently, and patiently transplanting seeds in the dark. Duke was well on his way to recovery with trust in love again.

On a midsummer day, Lillian, Harold's four-year-old daughter, was playing outside as her father tended to the farm. Hannah was inside, preparing dinner. Lillian was tossing her doll all over the yard.

Hannah had just glanced out the window to check on her before setting the table.

Lillian's hand slipped throwing the doll off to the side into the pond. Quickly glancing around for help, she told herself that she should get it. The doll floated around the water, teasing her, as she reached for it on the shore.

Ralph and Frannie *quacked* loudly to notify all the farm animals of the danger as Lillian slipped into the water. Gasping for air while going under the water made it hard for her to yell out to anyone. Duke was the first to make it there, rushing in with no hesitation to grab her and pull her out to safety.

In such a hurry, water had splashed down Duke's windpipe, but he was already committed to saving Lillian's life. Dukes struggled to pull her to shore as he choked on the water. In the whole disturbance of the rescue mission, an old, rusty piece of wire fencing sticking out of the ground under the water had grabbed hold of Duke's tail. He yelped in pain, flushing more water into his lungs as Chewy jumped in to help. Sir Chewy pulled Lillian onto the shore and licked her face until she responded, but by that time, it was too late. She didn't respond, and Duke had drowned in the pond.

The farm was never the same. The guilt force kept Duke earthbound, feeling shame that he didn't complete his mission. The souls of Harold's dad, Duke, and other lives lost on the farm that hadn't crossed over made their presence known from time to time. Duke's soul stayed near in the water hole, making sure that the other kids stayed away from there for safety.

That winter Frannie had had enough of the sadness and pain hovering all over the pond. She couldn't help it not to help. Frannie went under water to bribe Duke to some jerky if he would swim into the light. She channeled his PTSD frequency to protect the sources descendants and position tribes in sacred direction. She stayed until she made sure that Duke crossed over. He finally did, along with Frannie. Ralph waited for her on shore where there was limited water beyond the frozen ice covering the pond.

Frannie's body rose to the top, stuck underneath a thick layer of ice. Ralph was devastated, frantically waddling to the porch, *quacking*, crying all the way there, causing a loud ruckus until someone acknowledged him.

Harold came out and asked what the fuss was about. He could only guess that the mallard wanted his help but didn't know how. Ralph waddled as quickly as he could back to the pond with Harold following behind.

When they got to the shore, Harold immediately noticed Frannie's body, dead under the ice. Harold sat with Ralph by the shore, telling him how sorry he was for him and that there was nothing he could do to help or make it better. He felt horrible. Harold was used to being able to help animals and nurse them back to health, but this was out of his hands. He didn't like the insecure feeling of not having the control over these situations. After a while, Harold went back into the house for the night, feeling the pain of poor Ralph, who lost his love and mate for life.

Harold prayed that night that Ralph and Frannie would be happily together again somehow. He prayed that they would find their paradise. And so they did.

The next morning, when Harold and Sir Chewy went out to do their chores, they walked past the pond to see Ralph floating next to Frannie under the frozen ice on their plan to succeed death.

PTSD

The process to sharing dreams has chosen the ones to translate
PTSD—Prior to Seeing Darkness, Performed the Sight of Day,
Projecting Time Sequences Disorganized by Past Trials Seeded Deep
and there they stayed, haunting the sleep of those with PTSD
A Place to Store Demons, a Path through Severed Doors comes
the Power to Sense the Darkness to heal what happened before
the Plot to Save Destiny became a Plan to See Differently,
to Play the Soul's Decision that was once left in submission,
is now reality. Light and Love to the Souls with PTSD
A Paranormal Trance of a Secret Dimension Pointing Tribes in
Safe Directions—Planning takes Seeing Disruption as Protecting
the Source's Descendants. Either way you look at it, Paranoia
Takes Sheep Down to see what's underneath the glitz and glam
who preaches that taking sides determines your background, and
world all around. We're practicing to see death as a part of me,
while participating transcended spirits deliberate the PTSD
The parental thoughts sacrificed down for solutions
unknown in this part of town. Please Trust Soul's Decision,
Plowing through Sacred Divisions, Planting Truth Seeds in
Depth for a clear Perspective to See Danger as a gift from
a Partnering Team Simultaneously Divided, united in the
chosen one's of PTSD—People Torn in Separate Dreams
Believe You, Me—I pray for you, a Place to Sing and Dance!
The new PTSD

CHAPTER 15

BS

Biological sadness was instilled in every flawed being on earth by losses of loved ones, unfinished business, fixed beliefs about "self" caused by traumatic experiences, fear of fear, and unhealed circumstances in the bloodline.

As Bob the Scribe translated different perspectives, Sarah paced the main floor of the farmhouse, looking out all the windows. She wasn't viewing outer space (or wherever they were headed) but different life stories of an eclectic variety of species and how they responded to their environment, given their circumstance.

There were basic stories with a light side and a dark side, helping every living spirit on Planet Earth. There were angels and spirit guides working around the clock, whispering in ears thoughts, ideas, guidance, suggestions, and adjusting to the choices and actions of individuals.

It was like watching the building of a system in progress forever growing, forever changing, and forever evolving; baby steps of a toddler coordinating and calculating what muscles to use, how much focus it took to make that next step, and angels from the baby's ancestors calmly encouraging them to stand back up and try it again.

Sarah watched the honey system, where everyone born into the hive instinctively knew their purpose, going right to work like a body at sleep running on autopilot.

She saw archangels, spirit guides, guardian angels, and earthbound souls who had set open portals from residual energy or connections from their own lives. They all traveled back and forth between realms and dimensions at the speed of light. Whenever a human, animalia, or plantae thought, spoke, prayed, visualized, or put out a wish, the energy was there as though they were bound by law to show up anytime, anywhere to support the energy of the space until another prayer or thoughts changed the energy force.

Sarah could see lives set on course for bipolar, schizophrenia, broken siblings, breast surgeries, and buried souls all in a painful thought system of depression and delusional thinking. All these people she was seeing were set at all different time eras from BC to present time on earth's standards, all showing traces within Sarah's bloodline, but some with loose ends.

She watched and felt young Mickey playing as a child. Angels and shadow spirits were with him every step, setting stones in direction of the next step on an infinite course of multiple possibilities and outcomes for his particular quest. It was only a matter of what voices he chose to listen to that would build a bridge for his journey of where he decided to go. Sarah saw the outcome of Mickey's life after war. She looked into the eyes of his enemy, thinking that in order to save hundreds, thousands, possibly even millions, he would have to kill him. As a soldier, you gotta do what you gotta do. *Don't we all?* Sarah thought out loud.

The scribe showed Sarah of Sonja and how every negative thought she had circulating through her bloodstream and brain cells corrupted her vortex, inhabited by dark, residual energy that set into cancer cells overtaking her body with acceptance of her chosen mind. Sonja projected diseased energy all around her, unconsciously infecting them with her inner turmoil.

She saw Dominic taking in energy from his sensei while learning to be the best martial artist he could be. He focused on the instructions of his higher ranking with his determined, enthusiastic spirit guides at his side, training with him and cheering him on. Sweat dripped on the floor on the dojo, leaving residual energy of Dominic's essence of seizing that moment. Darkness waited patiently in the shadows for any moment of negative thought that called for the negative presence and support.

Sarah walked to another window that was showing a teen-age girl, Amanda, coping with her overwhelming feelings of never accomplishing her parent's expectations, of not being enough for them and their standards. Amanda struggled to break through to the world she knew was here, the world of singing and dance.

The birthday surprise caught Sarah's attention. On a window normally facing west that she would look out to watch the sunsets over the hills of the farm, Sarah saw the eightieth birthday party she never made it to, in a way everyone else expected.

The decorations at the party were lovely, as Sarah put it. Dozens of circular tables were placed in front of an open bar in the back of the room. Three bar tenders awaited the guest's requests and were kept busy by the number of bodies who attended. One corner of the back was designated for the bar and mingling while the other corner displayed an exquisite food buffet, barbeque western style, in honor of Sarah's country flare.

The tables took up the majority of the room for the guests that came for the free food. Most of them were sitting with a sense of seclusion to camouflage into a table setting where the little screen of their cellular devices could distract them from the uncomfortable feeling of communicating with another human.

In front of the tables was a small but cozy dance floor being taken up by senior, traditional couples, embracing the opportunity to sway and snuggle. Then there were the young children ranging from toddlers to five years old as well, "if you can walk, you can dance" age, mingling in with the oldest generation.

The front of the dance floor was a stage, mostly decorated with bouquets of wildflowers accented with red sunflowers, which were Sarah's favorite. A podium was set in the middle for speeches and announcements.

Leo walked in through the double doors in between the bar and buffet. He looked around, feeling quite uncomfortable. He recognized Sarah's daughters, Evelyn and Monica, who stood on opposite sides of the massive banquet room.

From Sarah's point of view, she saw both hands giving and receiving energy of every being in the room, including the spiritual realm. That room was crowded, jam-packed with humans, spirits, and natural energy waves, frequencies, and vibrations that connected us all. She watched Leo become flushed when he couldn't see Sarah, Patrick, or Dante, the three people that he would know that could make him feel welcome.

The spiritual realm was mostly busy as humans discussed their judgments, opinions, and fixed beliefs of others in the room; even their opinions of the three that had yet to show up were being insulted by judgments. As the two remaining siblings, the superior sisters, based on their "sick and wrong" prejudices of their own brother, Patrick, discussed the luxuries of their lives to whoever would gather around to listen, mostly in-laws and women who could relate to that kind of gossip.

Evelyn threw in remarks about Monica being on her third marriage and how "that poor woman will never figure it out." She told a small group circled up around her while ignoring all the children in the room along with their teenagers on their cell phones, not engaging in the party. Some of the teenagers formed groups with their special clicks to do the same thing their parents were doing, talking about the other family that was not just like them, feeling superior above them all.

With as much lighting as there was to shine on a big bright room, this room was dim. Shadows were passing to and through everyone, gossiping with ill intentions. If one person even spoke the name of another, the shadows would fly to that individual in the room and mimic the gesture to the other like a mirror. Very few on their cell phones would look up at the party to see who was around them, to find out where that random thought or vision came from. A couple of kids did look up from their phones when whispers of spirits breezed pass them. Instantly they noted in their minds that they were alone with their phone and brushed off the suggestion that someone was directing and projecting energy to them. Many calls were unanswered while other calls were being fed by more gossip.

The sisters were oblivious that when they spoke of the other, that energy between them was building a dark bridge between them by each side meeting in the middle. They were stuck in a cycle of not only pointing fingers but pushing fingers into backstabbing wounds, strengthening the pain between them, deepening with every puncture until it tore through a hole in the souls.

Monica returned the backstabbing with a bitch-slap of a comment from the other side of the room to her group of gossipers. "It's no wonder why her husband cheats on her. Look at how much attention she gives him. It's all about her."

Evelyn's husband, Norman, mingled casually with a few acquaintances by the bar. He swallowed a shot of scotch as he turned around, catching a whiff of, "It's all about her," pass by him, implanting disgusted thoughts toward his own wife. He leaned back against the bar, watching her laugh, having fun, blowing energy smoke to everyone in the room that she felt was less than her superior self, thriving off her insecurities. *What about me?* he thought.

Leo already had his fair share of Evelyn and Monica's energy exchange and didn't bring his necklace of garlic cloves to keep the vampires at bay. He sought out Norman at the bar that was coping with the dense forces in the room with alcohol.

Norman saw Leo approaching through the corner of his eye. Recognizing his presence immediately flushed through Norman like a sigh of relief. He nearly went limp as his shoulders dropped the tension out of his physical body, embracing Leo's conscious energy. Norman smiled, putting out his hand as a kind, welcoming acknowledgement of a traditional handshake. Norman's energy quickly shifted to be present with Leo.

"How are you, my friend?" Leo initiated conversation.

"I'm hanging in there day by day."

They briefly discussed Norman and Evelyn's family and new arrivals of grandchildren before Leo felt an overwhelming nervousness in his solar plex. "Where are Ms. Sarah and the boys? I wasn't going to come, but I decided last minute to support the celebration. We never know how many more birthdays Ms. Sarah will have. I was held back in traffic, so they should have made it here before me."

Norman connected strongly with Leo's feeling, as he lost his teenage daughter unexpectedly. He knew the feeling of precious time. "I don't know. I haven't heard anything," Norm said, shrugging his shoulders. "They definitely should have been here by now." They both looked around curiously.

Evelyn took notes on her husband's whereabouts, saw him talking with Leo, and demanded to know where her mother was. She stomped over to the middle of Norm and Leo so that neither one had a choice but to see her and acknowledge her.

"Where is my mother and Patrick?"

"They left before I did," Leo said, still looking around, avoiding eye contact with her and rubbing off the toxic essence she radiated. Leo stepped back for breathing room. That moment flashed a vision through Leo:

A Cadillac smashed into the back of a semitruck he passed in Murfreesboro; although the flashing lights of police, ambulance, fire trucks, and road flares hadn't grabbed his attention to notice that his chosen family was burning in a blazing car fire on the side of the road. How did he not notice?

Leo shook off the vision fed to him by his spirit guide. "No, it can't be," he said to himself. "That can't happen to Ms. Sarah on her birthday. No, it isn't so." He struggled to convince himself, but knew in his heart.

Leo's spirit guide, along with Norman's and Evelyn's, stood by patiently as Evelyn's phone rang. The call was coming from Patrick's phone. With a slight hesitation, Evelyn accepted the call. It was the Murfreesboro Police Department calling the last phone exchange from a device found on the ground near the wreck that had been ejected from the vehicle with Dante.

Evelyn turned ghost white, glancing back and forth to Norm and Leo. Her eyes started to cloud, overlooking sight of anything else around her, including herself. She couldn't keep herself standing. Tension in her muscles unraveled, slipping the phone right out of her hand. Guilt forces tugged at her heartstrings, pulling her to the ground.

Leo's mind acknowledged the vision of the wreckage as a piece to this night's story in just enough time to reach out and catch Evelyn from falling to the floor. Grabbing at her chest, she went limp like a rag doll, hanging in Leo's arms. Norm helped hold her as commotion started among the room.

Monica rushed through the crowd to get to her sister as quickly as she could. Monica had taken on character from Sarah about caring for other lives and had been a nurse for over twenty-five years.

"She's having a stroke," Norm blurted out to the crowd for any help.

Teenagers and young adults were already recording the emergency on their phones, but not one calling 911.

As Monica made her way through the tables of diners and watchers, the shadow of energy within her slipped away, fading behind her like ashes of a phoenix. This wasn't just Nurse Monica coming to assist; that was her big sister, and who else could she look up to if not for her closest sibling? Monica as she knew herself was no longer there. It was pure love determined to help. With her clear intention, Monica and Evelyn's connections with each other and extension in the room went from being selfish to becoming selfless.

Machines kept a steady beat of Evelyn's heart being monitored while lying in a hospital bed, unconscious. Norman slouched in a chair near the bed, emotionally and physically exhausted. Next to his spirit guide standing by, Norm's closest deceased family stood around him, sending warm, comforting intentions. He sat bent forward with his hands holding up his head. Something reached out, touching Norm's shoulder.

"In my experience here, I've learned that it helps if you talk to her. Let her know you're here for her," Monica said, set up in her nurse scrubs, handing Norm a cup of coffee from a vending machine down the hall.

"Is that so?" he questioned.

They had never gone to any church nor spoke about religious beliefs in any of their thirty-three years of marriage. Not necessarily nonbelievers, they were just too caught up in the fast pace of the world still waiting for sure signs on what to believe in.

"Oh, yes," she said, glancing over Evelyn's monitor. "It's unbelievable what I've seen the human body go through and make miraculous recoveries. Believing is seeing."

Monica stood at the bottom of her bed, praying for her big sister to make it through this so that she could patch things up with her, come clean with all the bullshit talk, and rebuild sisterhood. If only they were given another chance. Norm was feeling the same vibes of forgiveness and change.

Past thoughts and judgments died down as Monica and Norman focused on the healing of their sister and wife. Love and light poured out of them as they sent out intentions of her healing.

"Monica?" he asked.

"Yes."

"Do you think she will make it through this?"

She shrugged. "That is not in my power to say. Time will tell. In the meantime, pray."

The window screen shut off like a television. Sarah turned around to Roger/Charlie and Bob, the scribe. *Will I ever see them again?* she asked.

Roger and Charlie stepped in to explain. *When we got married, I smuggled a book from the waiting room of my office building to read to Patrick called* Love You Forever, *written by Robert Munsch.*

Sarah remembered this book. In fact, she liked it so much, when her mother was in a nursing home, Sarah and Patrick took a trip up to Kansas City for a visit before she passed, bringing the book to share with her.

Roger knew that book would spark her memory to that moment that had flashed on the windows screens instantly.

Patrick was twelve years old. Monica had just left for college, and Evelyn was already married. Patrick had seen his grandma a few times before, but only when they made the trip all the way to Missouri. Sarah and her siblings drifted off, only keeping in touch around birthdays and holidays. She realized she didn't want to feel detached from her mom like she felt as a teenager so long ago.

After experiencing the death of a husband, then remarrying, she understood a part of her mother's journey and was able to heal the resentment of bringing in a new parental unit. With losing a child as well, Sarah hit the realization of how precious time was and made more visits to soak in every moment she had with her mother. Patrick enjoyed every minute of it.

At the end of her mom's time on earth, Sarah and Patrick had come up for a visit with the book. Patrick insisted on reading it to her, not only show off his skills for reading but he found the story fascinating.

It was about a mother and her baby starting a cycle of mother's care for the baby, and the baby ended up growing and taking care of his mommy. The mother would speak to her child affirmations when tucking him to bed, when he made a mess, before school, etc. The mother would say, "I'll love you forever. I'll like you for always. As long as I'm living, my baby you'll be." Such beautiful words spoken for a child and parent to remember and feel, they thought.

Patrick read this book to his grandma a dozen times in one day, but Sarah just noticed something interesting when watching her life on playback.

At the end of the story, when the boy grew up and had a child of his own, he brought his elderly mother to his home to live with them so that he could make sure she was taken care of by someone who loved her because she, at one time, took care of him when he didn't know how to do himself. Sarah knew she should have brought her mom home with her on that trip, but hesitated to do so. Beyond the guilt force Sarah could feel, she kept watching to see what else happened right in front of her that she was too distracted to see at the time.

Whenever Patrick would read, he would say, "I'll love you forever. I'll like you for always. Forever and always, your baby I'll be, and forever and always, my mother you'll be."

He switched the words, Sarah thought out loud. The scribe rewound the scene on the screen. This time watching it, Sarah saw a new realm in the nursing room with them. As Sarah's mom sat up in bed, listening gratefully and patiently to the same story again, a gentle peace surrounded them. Ancestors, angels, and guides were in the room with them. Patrick's spirit guide whispered in his ear as he was reading. He listened.

Sarah felt an overwhelming sense of motherly love and pride of her lovingly instinctive child.

You are forgiven, Bob said as he turned off the window screens.

CAME TO BELIEVE

Mind over matter, faith over fear / force of nature guides
me here. The higher power awakens the darkest hour.
Digging in deeper, sleeping with night lights /feeling relief.
Embracing the darkness, I came to believe in myself—
digging deeper to the end of my rope. I lost control,
left with hope in something more than myself.
Step by step I pray to see the skies unfolding into me.
How rare am I holding this dream? / Coming this far
I came to believe, however I live, God agrees.
I pull myself—light and fire underneath / I
pull myself higher and God agrees.
Shooting star in the sky, digging deeper, flying high to the dark side
of the moon / I see you in the night, the darkest hour praying for
light. All I can do is hold you tight—give all the love I have inside.
Come with me—come to believe in all that we're made of.
Beyond the science is magic living in you, believing in love.

CHAPTER 16

POA

In the solar system orbiting out around Betelgeuse is a galaxy uniting the Canis constellations. Similar to the Milky Way revolving like a spiral vortex within the realms of space are three constellations, Canis Major, Canis Minor, and Canis Manna rotating clockwise in a circular gravitational force. This is known as the Canis Triangle, like the pupil of an eye having three irises within a massive iris.

Sarah's farmhouse in the center of a snow globe descended into the atmosphere of POA, the main planet in Canis Manna, also known as Paradise of Animals, Palace oh'Animalia, Place of Attraction, Plants Observing Animals, Purpose of Allah, and the list goes on. POA was a great place to RIP—recalculate inner priorities or rejuvenate instinctive programming.

Inside Sarah's farmhouse lenses on the windows rolled down like a scroll from the outside, revealing POA. For Sarah, it looked like a peaceful orb of abundance. Soaring in the sky with the birds, Sarah gazed out the windows in rapture at the Planet of Adventure. Canis Manna encompassed all four seasons at once, like four perfect sections of a pie molded into a perfect circle.

They flew over the summer-solstice desert, measuring over one hundred times bigger than the Sahara. It was an oasis created by brilliance. Sage brush, cacti, and, palm trees grew abundantly for herbs, cool shade, and shelter for reptiles and amphibians living in harmony and cooperation. Lakes and water holes grew from the burnt-orange sand like they were made for each other. Partnered rain clouds hovered over every water hole, replenishing water usage with infinite production of supply.

Sarah swore she saw Cleopatra by the pyramids that were set up for housing facilities and cities that were dreamed up by every being that had ever been there. Tepees and tents mingled in with the peak-formed housing, decorating a diverse spectrum of living in such unfathomable terrain. Neighbors worked side by side equally, sharing tools, talents, and magic to help constructing a new cob-home community in the hot desert environment.

All these beings used every form of communication imaginable—trance channeling, telepathy, clairvoyance, scrying, kinesis, and acoustic levitation to move objects with sound. All species worked together, knowing it was for the evolution of the whole, which included their loved ones and their own evolvement, in preparation for their next lives.

Tibetan mastiffs, schnauzers, and Chihuahuas were the most frequent among the Canis Kingdom to RIP in the desert, again as equals to Homo sapiens, serpents, and all other species of the land. Sarah saw creatures that were mythical in the human world, things she had to process into acceptance of the infinite.

Sarah's snow globe expanded, opening up in such a way that fit the desert into the globe right outside her windows. Still within her orb, they floated into the fall plateaus.

Rams, lions, and centaurs and dragons took to the fall plateaus as a favorite gathering section for their lifestyle to recoup in between paths, along with hounds, retrievers, terriers, and the Great Danes who also preferred to refresh independent personalities in this realm. Aspen groves, willow tree, and an assortment of leaves changed colors in a cycle back to the original seed that morphed into trees and plants that Sarah had never seen before with colors like a psychedelic dream.

Layers upon layers of plateaus spread out the valley with rock staircases for climbing. The rocks formed solid bridges to explore the whole land with tunnels leading out to playground for all species to enjoy together, surrounded by fruit trees of everything imaginable, ready to harvest. Trees lined the alleyways of compact soil covered in yellow, orange, and red leaves to cottages, cabins, and tree houses shared by all in this preferred season, very welcoming to guests for holidays.

Coming to a pine and evergreen forest, Sarah spotted her first centaur sighting of a small family traveling with a herd of deer into the woods. The deer were helping the centaurs transition into a loving, natural environment with respect in place of fear, supporting the family in the training of trusting the outdoors again.

As Sarah's farmhouse snow globe crossed into the snowy mountains, the fall plateaus got sucked into the globe like they were absorbed from within. On the front side of the globe laid the desert, and the back was a stunning view of the fall plateaus enhancing its waterfall feature for tranquility.

Underneath the waterfall, mermaids and mermen helped the Newfoundland canines with swim-and-rescue training, assisting them with their passion for saving human lives from drowning. Loch Mess Monsters with family cheered on the side by the shore, supporting the growth of the whole. Dolphins jumped, diving in and out of the water, circling and swimming with their friends. In fact, everyone in and out of water was friends of dolphins. Even killer whales, the largest dolphins, were healing and communicating with humans and other beings that ever felt victimized by the ocean somehow. Forgiveness was the name of the game here.

Land and water showed no dividing of species, no jealousy among any species; just harmony and love were what made this planet thrive with the magical elements of all possible creation. The aura of this whole planet made aurora borealis appeared to be in dim lighting. No offense to the sights of earth, but these beings knew how to use their energy and intention to the fullest.

The evergreens in the winter mountains were a glorious sight for Sarah. She had lived in the Appalachian Mountains and visited the Rocky Mountains, but this was another world, literally. Snowcapped mountains stood anywhere from ten thousand feet to over fifty thousand feet peaks with canyons, trails, rivers, and lakes. Elevation was no deterrent to a place of unlimited thinking and capabilities. Especially when the assistance of the dragons was needed in the area, the higher peaks helped travel and accommodations for the gentle, giant beasts in the skies. Icebergs grew in the center of snow lake, which they considered the ocean.

Shepherds, huskies, Newfoundland, komondors, mammoths, and even Bigfoot loved the snow and water in the winter mountains. Sledding, snowshoeing, and skiing were popular hobbies that humans liked to share with their friends in this chilly resort. In every seasonal realm, Sarah saw species that she had heard of, but in stories, myths, and the ones that went extinct before her time. Bears shared lodging with dwarfs, humans, werecats and wolves—all of which were excellent at cuddling when it came to story time around the fireplace and nap time.

Sarah consciously agreed that she wanted in on that too. Like Pac-Man gobbling up the cherries, the globe opened up to another season. Sectioned off into thirds, a triangle of three seasons and climates lived within Sarah's orb now, clearing her sight to the spring meadows. It was the closest to Sarah's vision of heaven in image nation that she had ever encountered.

Enormous bees were gratefully welcomed around the wildflowers that laced the rolling hills with every color created, but more vibrant than human eyes had adapted to. All the blooming trees radiated auras, sweeping through the air under wings of butterflies of mind-blowing sizes and hybrid metamorphosis, birds chirping from peacocks, robins, finches, parrots, and eagles the size of a private jet.

Ancient trees grew hundreds of feet tall to accommodate nests alongside human tree houses, squirrels, and chipmunks. Collies, poodles, spaniels, Saint Bernards, and toy group of Canis enjoy a good frolic in the spring meadows portion of POA. Hybrid elves tended to play with evolved sheep, goats, cats, horses, and monkeys that roamed the hills with a small town's custom to everyone that knew everyone.

"Is that... Are those..." Sarah stared at what she knew to be extraterrestrial beings blended in to the likes of all the diversity.

All kinds of creatures were helping with crops. The animalia kingdom donated their processed food to the fields as human hybrids gratefully embraced manure and feces dropping from the asses of any creature's contribution. The communities loved gathering for meals. It was even rumored that Archangel Raphael, Elvis, Jesus, Bob Marley, and Buddha came to help heal the new wave of beings and simply enjoyed a visit to the spring meadows of POA. Her snow globe embraced this immediately as if time never existed of earthly seasons. They all came together all in one and one in all, one planet, one being, one snow globe, one orb.

Farmhouses, ranches, and family communities built camp in the season to start the harvest cycling harmony around the whole planet. It was like time had never existed. If earthlings believed that smart phones, smart houses, and electric cars were high tech, they ain't seen nothing yet! From cavemen dwellings to ships in the sky, anything was possible here. Sarah didn't know where to start with her adventure but in awe and then take it as she went.

Her snow globe landed on top of a small hill overlooking a three-acre pond among hundreds in the spring-meadows quadrant for the planet. The snow-globe orb popped like a bubble immediately when it hit surface, leaving Sarah's yard outside her farmhouse with a giant desert sandbox to the north, plateaus of fall trees in the south, snowcapped mountains to her west, and spring rolling meadows on her east side. A cycle of seasons surrounded Sarah's farmhouse.

She marveled in excitement and gratitude, hugging Roger/Charlie while jumping up and down as if her elderly, horse-like body was not in question. She felt like a kid again. She felt her energy field as a space for her unique contribution of cocreating heaven on POA, rippling out to heaven in the universe.

Anything you need is here, Sarah, explained the scribe. *Your mission here at POA, if you choose to accept it, is to find your balance. We recommend you spend the "time" like it is currency. Gather with your loved ones, garden and walk with horses, rest and reflection, and service.*

How can I serve? Sarah wondered.

Bob replied, *Your expertise in genealogy will come in handy. The fact is, right now our main objective is the cleansing, healing, and replenishing of Planet Earth. The humans need help with evolving from all species and plantae. The corruption and wars between human versus human, human versus animalia, and human versus plantae are on the verge of destruction and even extinction. There are species and planets out there that are not too happy with what the humans have done to their families that were so graciously donated to earth in contribution of the whole. Some species want to take humans out of the whole equation because of the infection of consciousness that is overtaking the planet, not only torturing their loved ones on earth due to indifference but the dominate, superior attitudes that corrupt the hive mind.*

Sarah understood the challenges of being human. She now remembered what unconditional love was and how "to be" it. She felt like a medium still holding onto faith in the Homo sapiens kingdom. Bob continued to explain optimistically.

Fortunately, the Almighty has a plan. We need to gather the twelve tribes to our safe-haven rendezvous points before annihilation. We need you to gather the black sheep, the adopted chosen ones, and families connected beyond blood, the forever families connected by love. Every species that lives on POA have connections to life on Planet Earth that were earned through love and selflessness. Like the day you passed on from there, the birds spoke on your behalf. They vouched for you and sent the message out all the way to their spirit guides to their planets, allowing you safe passage on your travels through the cosmos. Your generosity has brought you here now.

To Sarah, that sounded like a dream job. There was only one problem for her.

How do I do that here? she asked.

Together Sarah, Bob, and Roger/Charlie walked out onto the front porch were there waited Jynx and Cleo, the fraternal twin were-cats that Sarah fostered in Florida.

Jynx had long hair of orange, brown, and cream swirled together in a smooth transition like a blurry, abstract painting. Cleo was a short-hair tiger tabby with a white collar trailing down her neck into her chest. Their humanlike bodies were clothed in cargo khakis and Bermuda shorts with floral-print shirts like they were Hawaiian tourists.

What in this realm of the universe are you wearing? Oh, for the love of everything sacred, I'm so happy to see you two again! Sarah shouted, embracing them so tight, which illuminated everyone's light around them.

Roger took joy in the reunion as well, cuddling his head into the huddle. The scribe interrupted the group hug after twenty seconds, at which the point of illumination in auras reversed conscious cycles in Sarah toward the healing process. Healing one helped the healing of all, and it showed.

They have been preparing your seat at the Flocking Tower.

Sarah interrupted him, *What kind of tower?* She giggled. Bob was pointing above their heads.

Along with three visible moons hovering over spring meadows was a circular structure, like a UFO that appeared to be floating in the air one thousand feet, with transparent elevation shuttles directly underneath.

All forms of life walking on the paths stopped in front of the clear portals. Some beings and energy fields just appeared from out of nowhere because their level of consciousness made it easier for travel.

It was as if the invisible tunnels detected the auras of the beings. As soon as they stepped up for recognition, a translucent beam of light shined down like UFO abductions, matching the exact color of the beings to the shuttle's energy. Once the light from the tower connected to the individual, a harmonic tone raised their bodies or energy fields through the air, ascending them up to the base.

That's the Flocking Tower, Bob pointed out as giant birds circled around the top, waiting for landing clearance. *That is where most of the work happens.*

Sarah clarified, *Oh, flocking... It sounded like you said something else.*

The group walked through the fields around the farmhouse on the path to the tower entrance. Jynx and Cleo explained on the way about their transitioning from cat to human. A human experience was in the cards for their reincarnated selves. Surprising to Sarah, in their next lives, they would all live together again in different forms and species—a rearranged new perfect moment and place of birth in this magically aligned quantum universe. Sarah looked forward to that life with her loved ones again even though her loved ones were there with her.

They arrived at the sheer elevators.

What's the trick here? Sarah wondered.

No tricks, the scribe explained. *You will know what to do at every bridge you cross. Like human life, you know what to do. You have instincts. Your spirit is whole. It always has been. It's the bruised and scarred mind that needs the rehabilitation. All you have to do is be you.*

Sarah stared straight up to the tower floating above her.

Leading by example, Jynx and Cleo stepped into the clear elevators. Immediately a golden-yellow light beamed down on Jynx, and a smoky-magenta color for Cleo. The light hit the chest of their bodies like a hook in a fish's mouth, circling around, releasing their vibrations willingly. By the sound of the tones pulling them up to the tower, Sarah would guess that Jynx was a bass and Cleo a soprano. Their pitch harmonized together as they levitated quickly up the shuttle.

Now it was Sarah's turn. Roger/Charlie stepped into the portal next to her at the same time. Sarah didn't feel any different other than light. If she had a body before, she couldn't tell anymore. A dusty-rose light came down to Sarah as a glittering indigo blue reached down to Roger/Charlie.

Sarah had decided to trust the process, fully surrendering to this familiar energy she hadn't felt since before she was born a human. The force that blew the wind, rotated the planets, moons, and suns, creates and manifests through thoughts and emotions revived Sarah in such a profound way she felt her tail rising.

When the blushing tint touched her core, another pile of manure dropped in the portal. Sarah thought more of it than anyone around her that were already adapted to love and acceptance with clear conscious of divine order. Sarah was the one in need of accepting herself however she was.

She opened her mouth to ask, *Why does this keep happening to me?* Locking into an E minor tone, Sarah ascended to the tower.

Processing is a process! she heard the scribe express as she got sucked up the quantum tube.

BUILDING BURNT BRIDGES

Deeper colors, deeper undercover / eyes adjust to the night
waiting for a full moon / wishing for the light. It's a beautiful
view I enjoyed with you / now taken out of sight
Take my hand—Angel in memories / Take my hand—
hold on as long as long as we can / knowing this bridge
was built on land—If we can't see it now, someday we'll
understand. We are the bridge—take my hand
Deeper oceans, stronger emotions / climbing to unknown heights
diving in the deep blue / ready for a fight. A new point of view
I can see through you. Who cares who's wrong or right?
Reaching out to what we're made of / pulling
through together forever in love. Holding onto
you, building this bridge—we rise above
Only scars apart / stitched by our hearts / mended stronger
than what we thought we are. Once burned by our hot
headed heat—cooled down by the waters underneath

CHAPTER 17

Code Red

Inside the tower was a world within another world. Sarah's family, friends, pets and anyone she ever knew in every life had an arrangement, their own mission in the Flocking Tower. She was greeted with love, light, and warmth radiated from everyone she passed as the scribe escorted Sarah and her small group to their area. Circular windows surrounded the tower with a view out on every level, inside and out, like glass walls, but unbreakable. The elements that made up this hovering structure were far more advanced than anything man-made.

Every species, hybrids, and orbs of energy were working, moving through the tower with a sense of urgency. A siren was heard in the background, coming closer to them as they walked through the tower. Sarah noticed the scribe sped up his pace.

Sarah glanced into rooms as they passed by.

This is the USE section of the flock—United Species Experiment. This quadrant tests ideas of the consciousness before it reaches back to earth to determine possible outcomes for humans. It helps create boundaries between species before one or the other crosses the line, Bob explained.

How is that going? Sarah questioned.

It's a process, but that's how we can relay back to the spirit guides and angels to help direct the best possible outcome for all that is involved in all the decisions fate has made.

She watched in rooms having small models of the Planet Earth exploding, melting, disintegrating through chemicals, drying up;

and one that surprised Sarah the most was a whole world at war with each other. Civil wars broke out within countries, leaving every man/species for themselves, killing each other for a can of beans or a loaf of bread; the blood of the bodies left on the ground without proper disposal; population decreased to five hundred million people to balance nature, cleansing the earth in a visually destructive way; and yet no humans or animals were harmed in the rehearsal of their own death.

Roger replied, *We pulled you all out before it gets worse. Free will has turned into sick and ill intentions toward each other, animal and tree slaughters, and domination filling a world meant for balance and equality as we are meant to be.* Sarah nodded in agreement. He continued, *As much as we need human angels right now, we also need the work of the other side, physical and nonphysical flow at balance and in harmony with the other. We tried inspiring humans with the yin-yang symbol to represent the goal of balance, but most take it on now as simple decoration, not embracing the true meaning behind it. While nothing on earth is meaningless, humans have become desensitized to every symbol, sign, and hint that spirit guides are presenting to them.*

Every quadrant of the tower had a divider hallway that led to the center auditorium, like a concert hall. Sarah's curiousness took her attention down those walkways where she could hear activity coming from. The group turned down the passageway toward the center.

What can we do to change this? she asked.

Cleo spoke up, *Unfortunately, we can't change the past. Nor may we interrupt free will and choice, so we are going to do what we can to influence the tribes to gather up to form new communities around the world to replenish the earth again with a new wave of human hybrids that will learn to live in harmony with nature. We spare the least corrupted, teachable, and willing to give up their ways that aren't destructive to the whole earth. The meek, selfless, and love-driven shall inherit the planet. It is a new time of BC—beyond consciousness is the theme for the new world.*

A commotion began to get louder as they approached the auditorium. Sarah pondered that concept. *On one hand, that sounds like a great plan. On the other, that would mean death and demolition to the majority of the population. Did humans bring this on themselves?*

Oblivious to consequence and synchronization, humans do have power over their fate, but no power over the reaction to their actions. The scribe described, *Most humans believe that they are too busy to take precious time to tap into consciousness, unaware of daily thoughts that form their everyday results. Ill feelings are passed down and taught to the children within their own bloodline and in their communities around them, accumulating unconsciously a connected decision to self-preserve by self-destructing. The majority of Homo sapiens on earth developed feelings of aloneness, expecting solitary results, then complain about being alone while pushing loved ones away or keeping them at arm's reach, thinking about killing others or themselves. No one cares about life anymore, unless it threatens theirs. It's a vicious cycle that celestial beings bound by universal law have to accommodate. So, yes, humans have brought this on themselves. They subconsciously wish for it every day but won't admit to it.*

Sarah shook her head in confusion. *In a world that doesn't make sense, contradicting everything, that somehow makes sense.* Sarah thought about that briefly as they came upon the auditorium.

Bob chimed back in, *Blaming gods and blasphemy is a challenge for humans, unaccountable humans, that is.*

Gods? Sarah emphasized the plural.

Yes. Humans have their Greek gods, Roman gods, Norseman gods, Egyptian gods, and the Christian God among other ancient idles. Humans have handed over the shame to the gods but want the power and credit for the pleasing manifestations, while some rely on FATE.

The group walked up to a giant archway to the center auditorium. It was grand enough to house technology far beyond NASA, where nature and the nurturers came together in and with abundance. It was a city with no walls or doors. Feng Shui, if you will. One area had a section of techs working the dispatching of angels and archangels, like air traffic-control pilots.

Sarah spotted Patrick and Dante in that area. They waved, smiling across the way, like they could smell her out of a crowd. Before she could get a chance to go over to them, they turned back to the digital screens, screens that were all flashing red. It seemed like an exclamation moment to Sarah.

Welcome to FATE—From All Thoughts Everywhere. This is the hot spot where the plot thickens. This is the headquarters for manifestation, the place where things are created by thoughts, Bob told Sarah.

Among the parks, rehab centers, birds chirping, and company, Sarah kept her attention on the bright-red strobes of light flashing on and off in Patrick and Dante's section.

A wave of echoes flushed through the auditorium and back like walkie-talkies, stereo, and Bluetooth got caught up on the same frequency.

Suddenly, over the whole tower, there's a loud PPA—planetary public announcement—saying: "Code red, Planet Earth! Code red, Planet Earth! I repeat—code red, Planet Earth!"

The urgency and speed picked up instantly. Dispatchers were rapidly sending messages out to archangels and angels on Earth to prepare for a code red.

What's happening? Sarah asked in the same urgent attitude.

Jynx and Cleo quickly ran over to help Patrick and Dante's dispatching crew as the scribe led Sarah to her section.

With a sunroof opened up, an indoor/outdoor library of books, records, and prayers on ancient rocks, scrolls, books, and hologram messages that played out stories of any life that had ever lived and who would ever live were all around her.

By Earth's standards, we don't have much time. World War 3 is like no war this world has ever seen, and we are going to make sure that the protectors, healers, and artists are safe and protected. It is these souls that accepted the mission of peace during chaos, love over diversity, and passion for life, not lust, that usher the next generations to the planet. Do you remember the plague that took your life on earth in the 1600s? Bob reminded her.

Of course, right on course, Sarah replied.

Excuse the earthly Southern expression, but you ain't seen nothing yet, Ms. Sarah.

They came to an office setting in the library with an open space for the hologram visual stories.

This is your area, he announced.

A stage floor centered in the middle of the library stood in front of Sarah.

What do I do here? she wondered.

You DO, divine order. It's like playing baseball, Sarah. When you are playing out field, the second you hear the crack *of the bat colliding with the ball, the body instinctively knows the exact location where the ball is going and where the ball will land. Its trust, faith, all knowing, call it whatever you wish. You will know what to do. Divine order is programmed within all of us to perform our unique purpose instilled inside us. We are all part of the process progressing for evolution.*

Indeed, Sarah did know all this before she had her human experience, and she remembered now. So why was she questioning? Sarah glanced around the tower again. This time she noticed that everyone was excited, even joyful and enthusiastic, about this code red. There was no sense of panic or anxiety, just urgency with a side of peace of mind that everything was always okay. Sarah knew this wasn't their first rodeo. The vibe of the tower was supporting and positive about the code red.

Do you ever forget who you are, Sarah? Bob questioned her.

Distracted away from the silly, smiling faces working code reds with the confidence energy of the Almighty, Sarah turned to see Roger. Roger was as she knew him, the way he looked the night they met on Earth in their most previous life together. Charlie waged his tail next to him. Bob drew her attention to her own body that they were staring back at.

Sarah was standing on her own two feet. Her jaw dropped. *I didn't even notice. Oh my god! I must have been thinking about my horses so much that I turned into a centaur.* Sarah laughed at herself as a round table rose from the floor. She quickly shared a warm embrace with Roger and Charlie, separately.

The table was used like Sarah's dining-room table in her farmhouse. The top turned to a screen that flashed on to her ex-husband, Jonathon, looking just as he did the day he got onboard the plane. He was dressed in khaki corduroy pants, white button-up shirt, and a navy-blue blazer. *The typical '80s salesman*, she thought, reminiscing.

Jonathon stood on the side of the highway in the Nevada desert with a baby in a carrier. Sarah zoned in on the screen to see what he was up to. She knew there was a reason of her being exactly where she was at that exact moment in time, whatever time was. Her energy field lit up and sparkled with the unconditional love that she had been feeling since she left Earth.

PERFECT WORLD

It's just another story teller in this fairy tale refusing
to turn a page until I understood betrayal—countless
destinies with the same destination counting journeys
living through generations in this world.
It's all the same story born of God's glory. We're
playing our role on the stage—enjoy the show.
It's a give and take game of forgiveness to recreate and
love all difference, the perfect balance. Smile and be. Allah
lives in you as the same God lives in me. Every moment
seeing through your eyes—storms seem harsh, but it must
be done / watching at the crossroads, the center of the
sun, the center of the universe we all become the one.
We're sharing the beauty of space in time, bearing a duty in the hive
mind. It's a game of forgiveness we play a part in. We need to live
and let live the light within, live strong willed, and light hearted.
Imagine worlds within worlds coiled and circled, planted
in the perfect world reaching back to where we started—
breaking ground from the roots of the departed.
You are my sunshine, my black hole sunshine. You turn the
rain on to clear the day. You'll never know, dear, how much
you've done here—thank you for lighting the way!

CHAPTER 18

TSS—The Sacred Spell

Jonathon set the baby carrier down on a bench at a rest stop on the side of the freeway in the middle of the Nevada desert. He stretched his limbs, cracked his knuckles, and lifted a Spanish woven blanket that had shielded the baby from the sun. Smiling at the infant, he pulled out a bottle of milk from his baby bag and handed it to the small child. The little hands took the bottle as though it was born with the dexterity of an acrobatic cheetah.

"Thanks for sparing my fingers," Jonathon joked. The baby giggled.

He took a big breath and looked to the road behind him to reflect on sun setting to the west. He took another deep breath like he was taking in the last breath of the sun's energy for that day in space and time.

"Namaste," he expressed to the universe and turned around to the road ahead. "Are you ready, Nova-D? The world is ready for you… Well, ready or not. Here you come."

He knelt down, kissing his index, middle, and ring fingers. Then he pressed his fingers softly on her forehead over her third-eye chakra and dropped the cloth back over the carrier. He picked up the baby basket effortlessly, swaying her back and forth while he walked down the road. Speaking out loud, he gave her a blessing to keep with her in her life's journey.

"Here's the thing, my love. Here is a blessing to help you help the world rise above. Take this wisdom with you. Remember it in all that you do:

"If you have unfinished business from a past life, you will be drawn to your own residual energy patterns until they are broken and healed. Bury it in the one and only soul forever. Dissolve yourself to pure energy. Be all you can be. The power in your diamond eyes is a gift to help you rise. You are wise. You have rehearsed 'Trust the Universe,' the one song we all sing. Sing together, love one another, and do good and kind things above all others. We all want love, and love awaits you as you evolve, and as you evolve, we dissolve, melting into love."

Vehicles drove past them without hesitation, no intention to stop and help. Drivers didn't trust the situation, believing that it was a hitchhiker's trick to get in their car and murder them or rob them. Despite the passersby, Jonathon walked on, chanting his song.

"Helping others and loving others heals the soul within. When you heal and love within, you free yourself, which frees all of your ancestors that carried that weight and faced the same fate. You will free your children of the burdens, challenges, and fears. Heal within, and we all win here. Pick yourself up off the ground. There is more than enough love to go around far beyond infinity. Through your diamond eyes, you'll see. Be compassionate and there for each other because that is your future preparing you for another. Do your best. Step up your game every step, every pain you gain."

Baby Nova let out a little *weep* followed by a *woo*. Jonathon nodded his head, acknowledging the child's awareness. He continued on down the road and on with his prayer.

"It's okay though. We will be here for you. Remember the humble voices. We will protect you. Humans are a human medium with energy that pushes you higher to the next step and the energy waiting for you on that higher step, pulling you through. Surrender and let go. Be yourself. Wake up the soldier within. Spread your glow in harmony in a constant flow, cleansing the organs, serving their purpose in accordance to our song. Hand in hand, pulling through, we're all in tune. Keep holding onto me. Open up the acoustics, write the

155

sheet music, and play along. I bless you, child, in this universe, where we sing one song."

Nova interrupted with a tra-la-la. Jonathon couldn't help but to be entertained with the little baby's advanced sense of humor. He chuckled before focusing on the sacred spell he was casting on the child.

"If we were all a cell in the body, getting fixated on only helping ourselves, we become combustible. We get diseased. Travel around the whole body. Go beyond the question of courage into selflessness, the next step of the world's consciousness. Be the wave. Like the ebb and flow of the ocean, we all ride one wave onto the next. Some stay behind, some will stay by your side, but we're all at our own pace. Keep the faith, little sister. Trust the process, trust in what we're made of, and most importantly, trust in love. Quiet the riot that throws you to the ground. Silence the sounds and turn the tables around. Expect the unexpected, and forget what you once regretted. Get comfortable being uncomfortable. Forgive the pain. Dance in the rain. Know that the underground will take your shame. Embrace the space in between. Know nothing here is as it seems. It's all in the mind of what we all find. It's never too late to call on your fate. We're all part of the same dream. We're all parts of the great plan, and love is the theme."

Suddenly, as if their souls attached to one other, connected by the falling sun, came a light shining from both of them. Glowing in sync with one another, her golden light matched to his deep, glittering royal blue, like a hue in the twilight's sky. Colliding into one, a beam of neon-green energy rippled out from them across the earth into the cosmos.

They carried on down the road. With an innocent gentle voice of the blessed child, Nova finished off this part of the song.

"I found you in this foggy, dense hollow. I am here. I see you in yesterday's tomorrow. Let go of your fear. I will wait for you. I will follow the broken road. I will see it through until this golden thread we hang onto is stronger than me and you, pushing and pulling either side. We'll pull each other through. Give me your hand. Take me on this ride. I'm in everything we do. Forever colliding, forever intertwining. Forever is me loving you."

Jonathon noticed three dark shadows pass by them swiftly out of the corner of his eye. They kept their distance and went on up the road ahead of them, parking themselves off to the side on the next mountain pass. He saw Pharaoh and his two buddies observing them. Staying focused on the child's blessing she had just taken on into her consciousness, he hummed along with her chant, secretly calling on the angels' help.

Archangel Michael and Raphael appeared before Pharaoh and his men. Pharaoh put up his hands as if he was held at gunpoint.

I'm here to observe, that's all, Pharaoh declared.

Archangel Michael aimed his sword at Jonathon and the baby as it shot out a transparent web, circling them as a protective shield that no force but love could penetrate.

Among the outside action, Nova continued on, "They who love in spite of the TSS—toxic shock syndrome—that can hit the best of us, are the soul survivors. We are the ones who live to write the rest. We hear the voices calling. We lift our family falling from grace. We are one with the angels installing us with love as we face this place with all that we are made of. It's the way of survival. Get ready to welcome the new arrivals. Share yourself, but be prepared. Your spirit guides you as you go. Get ready. Get set… Here come the characters of the next show."

Jonathon received a message through his earpiece. "The time is now. We are a *go.*"

Jonathon turned around, seeing headlights slowly pulling over to offer them a ride. "This is it, kiddo. One last thing before we say farewell."

VOICES CALLING

Vortex rising at the speed of light / rising up trailing glory
throughout the bloodline—relieving stress, buried and
compressed / firing up adrenaline intertwined / unlocking
ancestors trapped inside my veins crossing the finish line / into
a new assignment designed from the origin of alignment
Voices calling from deep within / so go ahead, knock me
down again onto a solid ground of hands holding me up
to win again and again / waiting to rise me up / to keep me
from falling—laying in the arms of the voices calling
Take my breath /flow on forever /take my hands
/ pull this life wherever the next star aligns—
connecting the shape of the bloodline
Written in the stars / my life on the line / light up the night /
spit fire behind this comet flying through the heavens reaching
higher than this mighty wind / always grounded and taking
flight / holding on for dear life / claiming my birthright
Voices inside are coming—voices calling me / I hear you
I've been waiting on something to be passed down / passing
up the world around—caught in between water and fire / the
air I breathe is lifting me higher—from the earth I transpire

CHAPTER 19

Good Luck Fate

Planet Earth, present day
I-80, Nevada Desert

Richard and Anne Somerset drove east down the interstate in their brand-new minivan they had just purchased for their up-and-coming family. They were in their midthirties, still young and prime, with their first child, Peyton, a four-year-old boy passed out in his car seat directly behind Richard in the driver's seat.

It was a warm day, but the sun had just set, and the desert cold was waiting in the night ahead. It had been a long drive that day from the west coast. They were hoping to make it home that night.

There was minimal traffic in the area. The next city was Elko, about thirty miles away.

Up ahead, Jonathon walked down the side of the highway, headed in the same direction. He switched hands for a better grip to hold the baby carrier as if he had been walking for quite some time and wearing out.

Rich saw the lonely father up the road and pointed it out to Anne. "Look, honey."

She looked up from her crossword puzzle to see Jonathon walking with a baby, then over to Richard, who was already slowing down the car.

They pulled over in front of Jonathon, offering a ride. Richard got out of the van not only to help strap in the baby carrier for

159

Jonathon but also to check if there was a real baby in the carrier. He wanted to help. On the other hand, he wanted to keep his family safe as well. It made him feel better if he knew this man wasn't a serial killer they just willingly picked up in the desert.

The two kids laid asleep in the baby seats in the middle section; Jonathon sat behind in the very back.

Richard adjusted the rearview mirror to keep his eye on him, unsettled about his choice to give them a ride.

"Where are you headed?" Richard initiated conversation.

"The same place we are all headed." Jonathon tried to joke, but didn't go over well. "Hmm, tough crowd… It's kind of a 'been there, done that' type of thing. Now I'm everywhere, really."

Richard blew it off as small talk. "I hear ya." He related back as Anne piped in.

"Who is this little one?" she asked, referring to the baby onboard.

Jonathon leaned forward, folding up a blanket draping over the top of the carrier, revealing a beautiful Mexican-American girl barely one year old, calmly sleeping.

"This is Nova-D, named by her father, representing the new," Jonathon explained.

"Oh, she's not yours?" the concerned mother asked.

"No. Her parents were killed by border control during a riot at the wall. Nova was still in her mother's arms on the ground when I got to her."

As a new mother herself, Anne felt a deep sadness for the separation of mother and child. "That's terrible. So are you adopting her?"

"Oh no. That's not my area. I'm making sure she goes to the perfect family," Jonathon expressed.

"That's good," Richard said as Anne looked confused, concerned about their current circumstance. Something was missing, she felt.

"What does the *D* stand for?" Anne questioned.

"*D* is for diamond," Jonathon replied, quickly changing the subject. He reached out, softly rubbing Nova's head. "This girl is the change in the world, and no one knows how but her."

With all sorts of questions piling up, Anne and Rich tried to brush off these profound words uttered out of Jonathon's mouth.

"I didn't see a car or anything broken down back there. How did you two get out in the middle of desert?" Anne insisted on knowing.

Jonathon leaned back, smiling.

"Wrong place, wrong time?" Richard asked, trying to keep it as casual as possible.

Jonathon remained relaxed and confident in his skin, or energy field. "There is no such thing," Jonathon preached. "We are always in the perfect place at the perfect time. Perfect circumstances are debatable, but timing and placement is a whole other playing field of co-inside-ness. Do you think it was a coincidence that your mom won the lottery, Anne?"

She nervously grabbed Rich's free hand from the steering wheel, squeezing tight. "Déjà vu," she whispered to him.

Jonathon went on, "Or what about you, Richy? Do you feel blame, maybe lack of control, because of the late checkout from the hotel today because of Peyton throwing up all the sugar he consumed last night? Or that you were given a second chance in life? That all happened for a reason, down to the smile you felt inspired to give the cashier last night who was going to go home and commit suicide but didn't. It also happened to put you here right now at this perfect time, fulfilling purpose." Richard began to feel the nerves in the vehicle, mostly coming from Anne.

"I don't believe we got around to our names yet, buddy. Who are you, and what's your purpose here?" Richard nervously stated.

Jonathon's tone intended to calm down the vibrations and tension as much as he could due to the circumstance. "I'm glad you asked that question. I am an emissary of the Almighty, sent here as a messenger for humanity. In all essence, I am an emissary of God sent here as a loving, powerful, creative, passionate spirit being of light, walking hand in hand with the angels, serving all God's children by bringing forth inspiration and empowerment with Christ consciousness, creating a world of peace, unity, and abundance. And so it is."

"Oh boy!" Anne threw up her arms. Overwhelmed with emotion, she surrendered to the moment, feeling powerless.

"My name is Jonathon. And although you will remember this moment forever, you won't be able to tell anyone. At this day and age, they wouldn't believe you anyway. I know that you still have a long way to go. One day, sooner than your ego thinks, you will believe.

Anne interrupted, "Believe in what, in God? Are you an angel?"

Richard's calm demeanor settled in the moment for what it was, leaving him speechless.

Jonathon stared at Richard from the rearview mirror. "It's fascinating how a writer with so much words of wisdom to share is struck speechless right now, Richard."

Feelings triggered foggy memories inside Richard, sending him mentally off on a journey of reflection. *Why does this seem familiar to me?* He recalled his near-death experience when he met Anne.

The vehicle was silent for a moment to process. Anne did her best, struggling in this surrealism. "So are we driving you to give someone special a message because you broke your wings, or what? I don't understand."

"Well, first off, I don't have wings. I never have. Second, we go directly to the source, when possible."

Anne was slowly opening up to the realness, remembering her whole life had been surreal and quite miraculous.

"What source?" Richard interrupted.

"You. You are the source full of LUCK—*living under correct knowledge.* Before you interrupt with more questions that are irrelevant to the situation, hear this. With your family's lottery winnings, you need to gather up as much food, water, and survival supplies as possible for what is to come. As you question your purpose and beliefs, here is your answer. Get to the highest elevation you can to set up sanctuary. Protect the animals and humanity we send your way. You will be tested and tried in the name of love, but you have everything needed to accomplish it. It is written on record, your purpose. Remember always to trust the process, trust in love, listen to your spirit guides, and trust me when I say, you were born for this. You earned your position here in your past life. You are the best suited for it, and believe it or not, you already agreed to this before you came to earth. I'm here to remind you of that divine promise. Remember, there are no accidents, Dick."

In a childlike voice of Nova...

Eyes of an Angel

I have searched for your eyes—a lifetime. Viewing a dream now so close—so close to me. Take these eyes of mine and lay them beside you to see the same dream—dream of you and me. Take these hands and hold them tight. I will follow you— follow you to our dream come true.

I have searched in the skies—a lifetime. Viewing the stars now so close—so close to me. I close my eyes. I feel them inside me. I see the same stars—stars in me and you. Closed my heart to keep you warm inside this cold igloo— and melted into you.

I have searched in the wind—a lifetime. Viewing what seems to come and go—come back to me. Take this soul where it needs to go. Take me somewhere new—to see a new scene. It's something I need.

Give these eyes wings to fly—to see through eyes of an angel.

Show me what the angels see in me—show me the love inside. I have searched for this—a lifetime with nowhere left to hide. Viewing a dream now so close—so close to me, it is mine.

Richard and Anne were stunned speechless. Both of their spirit guides floating by their sides smiled at Jonathon, Anne's giving thumbs up while Richard's gave a golf clap. Jonathon could see and communicate with the guides who were whispering affirmations of truth resonating in their ears.

It was as if they had to shake off a trance, staring out the windshield at the paint strips passing by the middle of the road.

As soon as they could shake off the stun mode, Anne turned back again. "What do you mean? What is to come?" She stared blankly at the empty back seat. Jonathon was gone.

Baby Nova remained sleeping next to Peyton, but no Jonathon. He just vanished. Richard looked back in the rearview and couldn't see him either.

Tires *squealed* as the van came to an abrupt stop on the side of the freeway. Richard and Anne got out of the van, opened the side door, checking on the kids, and to look for Jonathon. The loud screeches woke up both kids. Peyton woke up calm, but curious of the residual energy of Jonathon and new energy of the baby next to him. He stared tranquilly to Nova beside him. Anne rubbed her hand on Nova's chest, leaning into the back seat.

"It's all right, honey," she said to Peyton when something shiny caught her eye.

Nova slowly opened her eyelids, but the bright light of the minivan was beating right down on her, keeping them from opening for more than a second while adjusting out from dream world.

"He's nowhere to be seen," Richard said, climbing into the back seat.

Anne pushed a button, adjusting the indoor light of the van to dim slightly. "Oh my god, Rich, look at this!"

Shining brighter than the light in the van, Nova opened her big blue eyes. They were like a galactic supernova with flares spewing out glimmering shades of gold and indigo, but what really threw them off was, the shape of her irises were not circular.

Richard looked into her eyes and nearly fainted. An overwhelming burst of energy opened up in him. "Holy shit!" he said in a daze, staring at Nova's eyes. "There's no way in this world that is possible," he exclaimed as Anna blurted out, "Diamond eyes."

Not a vehicle was in sight except their van on the side of the road. A click away, standing in the sagebrush at the base of a mountain, were watchers. Pharaoh and his two men in black suits and bowler hats staked out the family, watching Richard and Anne trying to keep their cool on the side of the road.

The men's blood-red irises flipped lenses under the lids from binoculars, focused on the van, to stationary night vision. Earpieces in the shape of hearing aids blinked red in their left ears. Both men turned to each other, receiving the same memo, then over to Pharaoh.

Does Osiris know about this? one questioned.

A code red comes from the origin, or straight to the origin. Osiris is already preparing, Pharaoh answered. *Keep an eye on them.* He continued pointing to Richard and Anne.

Of course, his twin partners said in unison.

Pharaoh pushed in on his earpiece. *That's affirmative. Planet Earth, code red! I repeat. Planet Earth, code red!*

Archangel Michael and Raphael suddenly appeared before Pharaoh and his men as they all watched Richard and Anne drive away with the children.

In the land of POA—the Proof of Afterlife

The video screen shut off in front of Sarah. Instinctively she knew what to do. She could see what was going to happen in divine order, and the scribe was right. She ain't seen nothing yet. She knew the world would never be the same again. There was one life to live, one life at a time, but time was only numbers in sequence, optical illusions in our consciousness.

You see now, Sarah, love has no time line. Love made up my soul to fill your hole so you could see mine. It's all aligned in synchronized stories to be told for the evolvement of the whole. The scribe left Sarah to her purpose.

Who would tell the story of what was to come? Only the soul survivors knew.

Until the revealing, come what may.

COME WHAT MAY

Pulled back like a sling shot / fling me further than I've ever got—looking back I see the whole path / what's brought me here today… Here I go, letting go of yesterday—come what may. Praying for the best, living for today—come what may. Leaving my mark on the trails that paved my way—now come what may. Held back and burning hot / fire away, giving all I've got—digging deep, shooting past how far I've come today. Here it is, the day after yesterday—come what may. Hoping that the rest make it all the way—come what may. Leaving a spark with the tales I wrote along the way—now come what may. Different paces, different colors, all these faces facing each other—come what may and may it come with grace. Somehow we evolved this human race / killing one another, fighting for space. And here the God's watch in between stars with all the space in the world / Watching us all coming around full circle. Watching us running around full of doubt, checking the time like we're running out—come what may. We're all dying to save the day / come what may. Our human nature wants to stay / come what may. It's our fighting spirit living for today, letting go of yesterday—come what may. When we die, we lead the blind side / having been on the ride / we can change the tide for the one's coming our way—come what may.

ABOUT THE AUTHOR

Robyn Young was born in Washington state. She grew up in Utah. Her story is the spice of life with a variety of journeys through travel, jobs, and personal exploration. She saw herself as a certain person and chased her dreams in all that she does. She trained in martial arts, got her black belt, and became an instructor for a portion of her life. That in itself is a whole other story, but it opened her up to self-awareness and energy we project and have the power to change within ourselves to be all that we are to our highest potential.

As far back as she can remember, paranormal events, apparitions, and different realms of the universe have presented themselves to her in different ways to get her attention. After her father passed away, who was a poet, she has been inspired to write more and more about the visions she has seen, profound thoughts and voices we all have swirling around our heads, while wondering if we all have a shared consciousness. We all wonder about the afterlife as human beings, and the reason the author wrote this novel is to connect a story line with the theory that her wondering mind has conjured up in hopes to relate with anyone else wanting to take a journey about what may be going on around us that our human eyes don't see.

The author's wish for this novel and the world is to bring forth human, animal, and environmental connection, which her soul feels is an important aspect to our human experience. If anyone out there can relate to this story, may we all be conscious of our mindset and may we all change the world together for one and all.